BONES TALK TO ALL

Linda Thompson

BONESHAKER TRAIL
Copyright © 2008 Linda Thompson

ISBN-10: 1-897373-67-8
ISBN-13: 978-1-897373-67-5

All rights reserved. No part of this publication may be reproduced, stored in a retrieval system, or transmitted in any form or by any means—electronic, mechanical, photocopy, recording, or any other—except for brief quotations in printed reviews, without the prior permission of the publisher.

This book is a work of fiction. Names, characters, places, and incidents are the product of the author's imagination or are used fictitiously. Any resemblance to actual events, locales, or persons, living or dead, is coincidental.

Scripture quoted from the International Children's Bible®, copyright © 1986, 1988 by Word Publishing, a division of Thomas Nelson, Inc. Used by permission.

WORD ALIVE PRESS

Printed by Word Alive Press
131 Cordite Road, Winnipeg, MB R3W 1S1
www.wordalivepress.ca

"There is a right time for everything.
Everything on earth has its special season."

Ecclesiastes 3:1

CHAPTER 1

MATTHEW TIMMOTAY and his best buddy, Nathan, shuffled along a branch of the giant beech tree at the town's park entrance. They moaned with glee, because the cold wet bark sent icy shivers along their bare legs. They'd hungered for a warm spring day like today, especially after yesterday's flurries, and had jumped into summer shorts.

Matt focused his camera on Nathan's younger sister below them. "Sarah," he called, "move the front wheel to the right and lean forward." As a late afternoon wind blew her blonde hair over one shoulder, he pressed the shutter button.

He slid the camera down to Sarah by its strap. "Nathan, I'll print off the shots this weekend. I can help do the poster on Sunday. That'll be lots of time before your speech."

Nathan combed his hair. "Are you really skipping a speech this year?"

"I'm as good with speeches as you are with singing solos." He opened his mouth to say more but was interrupted by angry chatter above them. Not four feet away, a brown squirrel jerked its bushy tail and rested an arm against its hip. It looked like their English teacher, Mrs. Bailey—except for the tail, of course—when Matt told her that afternoon he'd decided to skip a speech this year.

As Matt and Nathan broke into peels of laughter, Sarah snapped a photograph.

Nathan had barely looked away from the squirrel when he gasped and pointed to Main Street. "My bike!"

Sure enough, a skinny teen in a black jacket whizzed past the park on Nathan's silver bicycle. Matt scrambled after Nathan to the lowest branch of the tree. He ignored the bark scraping his thigh as he jumped to the ground, but it burned as they raced to Matt's bicycle. With Nathan sitting double and clinging to his shirt, Matt's hands strained against the handlebars. He pumped the pedals with rock hard muscles, grinding the wheels through the gravel path.

When the tires made contact with the sidewalk, the chase held promise. He swung down Spicer Street, leaning into the brisk wind as did Nathan.

Matt pinned his eyes on the bicycle ahead. His father's old camcorder, swinging by its strap on the handlebar, bumped his knee. He tried to bump it gently.

Nathan groaned in Matt's ear. "Don't lose him. I want my bike back."

The Silver Bullet, as Nathan called his bicycle, swerved right and disappeared, but Matt knew the alley. Being the right-of-way to old Mr. Talbot's garage, it ran behind the doughnut shop where Nathan had won the bicycle two weeks ago.

Matt squeezed the hand brakes. He turned the wheel to follow, but when he saw the teen dismounting ahead, he swerved away from the alley.

"Stop," Nathan urged. "He didn't see us. He's talking to some girl with pink hair."

Matt braked. Before it stopped, Nathan slid off the bicycle. Hitching the camcorder over one shoulder, Matt joined Nathan at the corner of the building. The sun was setting and Matt shivered in the cool air.

A stout youth with square shoulders and a square face waddled into view to join the others. Matt spoke first. "Ball Cap. I should have known."

"I thought our problems were over when he graduated to Junior High," Nathan reasoned. "He must have recruited followers. Now they steal bikes."

Ball Cap didn't exactly waddle, but he was so stout that kids had been known to call out, "Quack, quack." It happened a lot the first year he and his family moved into town—until Ball Cap started to fight back. And he was good at fighting back.

The group of three huddled close together and shared some sort of fancy handshake. Matt whispered, "They're putting on gloves."

Nathan's eyes widened. "We have a gang in our town?"

"Sort of. Dad says Town Council calls them Wannabees."

The youths marched towards the doughnut shop and disappeared behind a metal garbage dumpster on the alley's right side. Nathan stepped forward into the giant shadows. He hugged the wall, hidden by the dumpster.

Goose bumps popped up along Matt's arms. "Don't go so close."

"Come on. They don't have x-ray vision." Nathan stepped around a mud puddle out of respect for his brand new neon-striped running shoes.

Matt hesitated, then followed. "I'm more concerned about their hearing. If they torture you to death, I'm not taking over the bike-a-thon."

"It's in your job description as Second-in-Command."

"Is not."

"Is so."

Matt peered through the space between the dumpster and the building's brick wall. He whispered, "I think they're going inside."

"Then I'm going for my bike." As Nathan stepped forward, the girl with pink hair shuffled back to the Silver Bullet. Nathan quickly pulled back and Matt held his breath until a gravelly voice said over her shoulder, "I can't do this with gloves on."

Pings ricocheted through the alley. It took a minute before Matt realized they had spray paint. Back against the building, he glared at the two boys through the crack. Tom owned the building. Everyone liked Tom. He'd handed out free doughnuts and hot chocolate a week ago when their class cleaned up the unused portion of the park's bicycle trail in preparation for next month's bike-a-thon.

Pink Hair walked up to Ball Cap. "The gloves are too big." Matt loosed the lens cover from his camcorder and switched the machine on. He zoomed the lens onto the two active painters and allowed the camera extra time to focus in the low light and narrow space.

He touched his thumb to the record button.

Ball Cap faced the camera. As Pink Hair spit out a colourful word, her paint can dropped and rolled towards the Silver Bullet. The complainer bowed her head over her left hand and she danced on the spot. Without warning, a door burst open and two garbage bags sailed through the air. Pink Hair ducked. Matt jumped.

Nathan jumped because Matt jumped. Shoving his glasses further up the bridge of his nose, he whispered, "What?"

Tom exited the shop with a garbage bag in each hand.

Everyone on camera froze for two seconds. As the Wannabees came to life first, paint cans dropped to the ground—except one that bounced off Tom's left shoulder. Ball Cap jumped onto a bicycle nearest him and sped left from the alley. Tom chased the other teen on foot to the right. Pink Hair bolted past Matt and Nathan huddled against the wall, and she never once looked back over her shoulder.

Matt clicked the camera off. Nathan darted to the Silver Bullet while Matt, his heart racing in outrage at the attack on Tom, scooped up a glove and paint can near the bicycle. As Nathan disappeared around the dumpster with his bicycle, Matt sprayed the seat and handlebars of the remaining bicycle. He whipped the can against the wall where the others lay. "There. Have some of your own medicine." After he stuffed the glove into his pocket, he snatched up the black jacket that Nathan had tossed from the Silver Bullet.

Nathan had Matt's bicycle upright for him by the time he joined him on the street. Nathan shook a foot. "I collided with the mud puddle, but at least I've got my bike—"

Staring over Matt's shoulder, he groaned.

Matt swung around, facing the direction of Nathan's stare. His legs turned to rubber.

The skinny teen raced towards them, screaming, "Put my bike down! Thieves! Someone call the police."

Matt's instincts howled danger. Not nearly as big and clumsy as Ball Cap, if the youth reached them they would be goners.

They hit the pedals. Matt's heart thundered in his ears and he broke into a sweat as he strained against an invisible elastic band. Pushing all his weight into a final pump, the wheels spun forward. He pedaled faster and faster. He sat down on the seat and shot a look over his shoulder. The youth had closed in on them at least half a block.

When Nathan glanced over his shoulder, Matt spotted alarm on his face. Both boys instantly stood up and rode for all their worth. The youth yelled again for the police. Matt knew if they stood any chance at all to lose this fellow, they had to split up. Did they have time to turn a corner before he reached them?

Two blocks down, with the true thief still in close pursuit, Matt panted, "You go left up here on Todd Street. Keep turning until you lose him, then come back out at the tracks. I'll meet you there in five minutes. We'll go to my house." He unrolled the jacket and held it out to his side.

"What are you doing?"

"I hope he loves his jacket more than the Silver Bullet."

"Okay. See you in five."

Matt glanced back. "He must work out to run like this."

Nathan slowed to turn left. "All the more reason to say *adios*."

Matt nodded, and he tossed the jacket towards the road's center as he swung right. With an eye over his shoulder, he saw the youth slow down at the intersection beside the jacket. When he saw him pick it up and throw it back down again, Matt's muscles relaxed.

He turned twice more while he caught his breath. He headed towards the train tracks. Recovery of the Silver

Bullet chased away a week of gloom caused by its theft. Triumph swelled in his chest as he imagined Nathan's elation. "Yes!" He knew that, for his friend, the bike-a-thon was back in order again.

He braked at the stop sign at Main. He slid a hand through his flattened brown hair and straightened it with what gel remained in it.

That's when he heard it. A whistle. A simple, gentle, train whistle.

Matt stared intently at the gray sky in the direction of the only tracks in town. Closer this time, the whistle sounded again. Faster, the whistle blew. Matt's heart rate picked up. Then, the whistle screamed through the air without pausing at all.

Sounds of squealing metal on metal ripped over and around the houses like a tidal wave. A dream-like fog swirled around Matt's vision and pressed close against his skin while his hearing deafened to a dull roar like ocean waves—except for the tremendous pounding of his heartbeat in his ears. Nathan had a history of racing trains.

Matt steered his bicycle towards the tracks, hardly aware the streetlights were flickering on. With feet like lead, he pedaled through the slowest time warp. Ahead, people ran onto the road toward the crossing gates. An acrid smell filled the air. Matt couldn't tell where it came from or even what it was.

Trains never stopped in their town.

Matt squinted at a white pick-up truck, parked sideways against the crossing gates. It spilled white smoke into the air, and a gust of black smoke swirled from behind a front tire. A silver bicycle twisted around its front wheel drew murmurs from people gathering there.

Matt's bicycle rolled to a stop. If Nathan was riding a silver bicycle, and another one lay here, had they taken one that didn't belong to Nathan after all?

The monster on the tracks rolled to a final stop. Forcing his legs to move, Matt slid off his bicycle and laid it down. His eyes searched for his friend. "Come on, Nathan. Right now. There's been a terrible accident here." Where was the rider of this bicycle? Why couldn't the distorted bicycle be red, black . . . any color, except silver?

Shouts rose on the other side of the train. People stood still and silent, their faces strained with severe lines. A man squatted to look under the train, so Matt squatted too.

His chest shuddered. Identifying the lump under the train, Matt gasped for air. A leg, with a muddy wet shoe attached, lay between the two tracks under the monster. Only a leg.

His eyes burned. On the other side of the train, feet hurried from one spot to another. Matt straightened up and forced his stiff legs forward. Nathan had to be waiting for him on that side. He stared at two railway cars for a long time, wondering if the giant would awaken while he crossed to the other side. However, it seemed paralyzed amidst the yelling. He crossed through.

Unlike where he'd come from, people here gathered into one cluster, fetching things, waving arms. One-worded shouts intensified about bleeding, ambulance, police, doctor. As if hearing their panic, the ambulance lights sped closer, a fire truck's beacon flashing directly behind them.

Matt squatted to the pavement to ward off a wave of nausea. Away from the crowd, on the road, lay a pair of eyeglasses. Nathan's eyeglasses.

He stared under the train at the neon-striped shoe. Nathan's leg lay under there.

The roar filled his ears again and his body twitched. He slumped to the ground where black fog blinded him fast and furiously.

When Matt opened his eyes, he struggled against the green plastic covering his nose and mouth. "It's okay, buddy," an attendant reassured him. "You fainted. Wear the oxygen for a few minutes."

A female police officer arrived with two blankets. She spread one over him with shaking hands. Matt's jaw shivered. "I'm so cold."

The attendant laid the second blanket over him. "Were you hit by the train or the truck?"

"No." His voice sounded far away, like his ears were stuffed with cotton balls. A wave of nausea rolled his stomach. He squeezed his eyes shut and tried to wake up again.

"I'm Officer Mary. Do you know the boy who was hit?"

Matt's mouth quivered, so he pressed his lips together. If he didn't say it, it wouldn't be true. Nathan might still come to meet him. He squeezed his eyes shut again, and with every fibre of his being he willed Nathan to walk over to them.

Officer Mary's cold hand touched his forehead. "We need to talk to his parents. It's very important."

Matt inhaled, forcing away some of the tightness in his chest. "I was meeting Nathan here. Nathan Nadeau."

Officer Mary nodded to someone. When footsteps moved away, Matt turned his head to look, but instead, watched the stretcher slide through the back doors of the ambulance. "Is he okay?"

How could he be okay with his leg under the train?

The attendant looked at the ambulance. "He's hurt pretty bad. How are you feeling now?"

"I have to go with him. He hates hospitals. He faints at the sight of blood."

Officer Mary nodded. "They won't let him see the blood. What's your name?"

Matt couldn't remember how long he stayed there. Officer Mary and another officer drove him home, still wrapped in blankets, and she talked to his parents. He'd seen the same look on their faces two years earlier when Uncle John had been killed in a car accident. Matt had only been eight years old, but he'd never forget that look. They'd lived with his dad's depression ever since.

Later, tucked in bed, his parents' voices muted in the bedroom across the hall, Matt stared at the ceiling. Looking at his bedside clock for the hundredth time, the numbers glowed that it was long past midnight.

Silence stretched across the house. The furnace clicked on and warm air pushed into his room through the floor vent. When the phone pierced the night, terror pierced Matt's whole body.

His parents' bedroom door opened and spilled light into the hall. Mom came to sit beside him, running a hand over his hair and filling his room with scents of perfumed soap.

Matt inhaled, wishing he was four years old again, snuggled on her lap. He opened his mouth, but a rapid fire of pictures paralyzed his voice. A bloody leg with a running shoe, a crumpled Silver Bullet, Nathan's eyeglasses on the road, Nathan on a stretcher. He closed his mouth.

His father's voice, deep and thick like that other night, broke the silence. "Nathan's dad phoned. Nathan's been in surgery. Now he's in Critical Care. There are a lot of machines keeping him . . . alive."

Matt whispered, "His leg?"

"He's lost both legs. Broken ribs have punctured his lungs and his heart is injured. But he's alive, Matt. That's a miracle."

"Was it the train or the truck?"

"The truck hit him into the path of the train. We're not sure yet of all the details."

Matt heaved. "I feel sick."

Chapter 2

NEARLY TWO DAYS had passed since the accident. Matt walked the house so often that his mother's eyebrows squeezed into worry lines every time he passed her. The evening news called it a "tragic accident in a little town west of the city that's left ten-year-old Nathan Nadeau fighting for his life." How did one fight for his life when he wasn't even conscious?

In spite of tossing and turning Friday night as he listened to rain pelt against the window and the wind howl, Matt woke on Saturday morning with the clearest head he'd felt since the accident. Although he hadn't heard any noises, the aroma of toast indicated his parents were up. It signalled the beginning of another day without Nathan.

The doorbell rang. Matt jumped out of bed and dashed downstairs as Mom set a cup of coffee on the table for Chuck Nadeau.

Chuck's whiskered face and rumpled shirt dashed Matt's anticipation of good news. "Good morning, Matt. I was telling your parents that Nathan had a rough day yesterday. His heart stopped twice."

Matt sank into a chair and tried to unknot his stomach by taking a deep breath. "Can I see him?"

Dad's spoon clattered onto the table. "I'm sure visitors have an age limit to a Critical Care Unit. You don't know what you'll see there."

Matt pushed aside visions of pale and lifeless bodies lying under stark white sheets row by row like a living morgue. "Nathan's my best friend. I want to see him."

Mom sat down at the table, but before she could add her own protest, Chuck slid a large brown envelope across the table to Matt. "It's because of that friendship we want you to take over the bike-a-thon. You know how important this is to Nathan. He loves his aunt with those triplets, and that building needs playground equipment for preschoolers more than ever. Nathan has already collected over a hundred dollars here."

Matt felt cold dread wash over him. He'd only ever promised to help Nathan, not be the organizer. He'd watched his dad in politics for as long as he could remember and people quickly blamed him for things he hadn't been part of. What if the bike-a-thon failed? It'd be his fault. What if he got depression like his dad?

Chuck's eyes glittered. He leaned on the table. "Those kids don't have much chance for this otherwise. Money's too tight on fixed incomes. While Nathan's learning to use his artificial legs, it'll do him good to know you did this for him when he couldn't."

"Nathan's an organizer. I'm not."

"Nathan trusts you."

"What about Sarah? She could do it."

"Sarah is only nine and has problems in school."

Problems? Telling Mrs. Bailey he wasn't doing a speech was a big problem, especially when the big kick-off for the bike-a-thon was a speech. This was complicated.

Dad interrupted. "Matt, why don't you take a few days to think it over?"

Matt looked at his dad, who had always been after him for procrastinating. The dread lifted away. He nodded. "All right. I'll think about it." He could come up with an excuse if he had a couple days to think of one.

Chuck left the envelope on the table near Matt.

Mom asked, "How does one acquire artificial legs?"

Matt fidgeted on his chair, half listening to Chuck. "The government will pay for standard legs. We'll buy him swimming legs. They cost a few thousand dollars."

Chuck drained his mug. Matt's urgency grew. "So will you call the hospital and ask if I can visit?"

At his father's nod, Matt rushed upstairs to brush his teeth and dress. By the time he returned, his father was pacing back and forth in the kitchen, running a nervous hand through his hair. Chuck shoved his hands into his pockets. He apologized. "I wasn't even thinking about your brother's accident. Why don't I take Matt to the hospital? I'll bring him home when he's ready. You don't have to go there."

"That's a lot of driving."

"I'm grateful Nathan's stable enough that I can leave the hospital for a while."

As Matt stood in the doorway, Dad's eyes darted between him and Chuck. Before Uncle John died, he'd spent two days on life support. Now, his father avoided hospitals altogether. Matt pointed to the calendar on the wall and said, "You have that meeting this morning anyway, Dad. I'll just go with Chuck." He left, walking out the front door so his father didn't have to make the decision.

HALF AN HOUR LATER, Nancy Nadeau swooped her arms around Matt outside the double doors of the Critical Care Unit. At the sight of her red, swollen eyes, he realized she'd done a lot of crying over two days.

Matt swallowed hard while Nancy rang a bell and identified herself by an intercom. "Don't let the noise scare you," urged Nancy.

As soon as the big door swung open, mechanical clatter surged through. In spite of Nancy's arm tight around his shoulder, he wobbled. Matt entered a room the size of the school gymnasium. He gawked at Machine City.

Nancy guided him left and set her purse down. That quickly, he stood at the end of Nathan's bed.

A young man dressed in a green uniform glanced at them over gold rimmed glasses.

He pushed a needle into a bag of clear fluid that hung on a pole beside the bed. "Hi Nancy. I'm giving him something to help his kidneys work better. Hello. You must be Matt."

Matt found it hard to talk when his tongue refused to move. He nodded. The man's name tag read, "Joel, RN."

While Joel dropped the needle into a plastic container on the wall and lifted a pen from his pocket, Matt forced his eyes to the bed. Except for Nathan's hair, uncombed and dirty, he couldn't find a single resemblance to his friend. Eyes bulged into tight lines. Nancy dodged a cloudy white tube taped to the side of his mouth as she kissed his cheek. The tube joined a hose which draped over the mattress to a machine beside the bed. Every few seconds the machine clicked, air swished through the hose, and Nathan's chest rose.

"Matt, my name is Joel and I'm Nathan's nurse today. Come closer and I'll explain the things attached to him."

Matt stumbled forward and his shoe squeaked against the flooring. He shook Joel's outstretched hand. First, Joel pointed to a box above the bed. "That monitor is like a computer screen. The top line shows us his heart rate, the second is blood pressure, and the third is oxygen levels. It's critical we keep these three stable because they keep us alive. These small pumps on the poles give him medication, blood products, and fluids because he can't eat right now. The machine on wheels is the respirator. It breathes for him"

One pump beeped and flashed a red light. Joel repositioned a thin tube attached to Nathan's arm. After he hit a reset button, he squatted beside the bed. Matt stepped back and studied the plastic devices hanging on the bed frame. "Lungs are like balloons, and broken ribs punctured his lungs. These boxes keep his lungs from collapsing."

"Where do the tubes go?"

Joel lifted the bed sheet. One tube, held by wide tape, disappeared into Nathan's chest. Matt gulped two really deep breaths and told himself fiercely he would not faint.

"Nathan has two of these. The one near his heart came out his morning."

"Is that a good sign?"

"It's going in the right direction."

The news said Nathan continued to fight for his life. What about the brain power behind this technology? What about the people who used it? Just as he counted the twelfth piece of equipment, the respirator bellowed a long harsh wail. Nancy hastened away from the bedside and Joel rushed towards the head. The monitor's third line flashed numbers in a dramatic drop from ninety to eighty to seventy. A second nurse slipped gloves over her hands and pulled equipment off the wall. Joel disconnected the hose from Nathan's mouth tube.

Nancy's eyes shifted between Nathan and the monitor while her fingers dug into Matthew's shoulder.

"When fluids block the tube, oxygen can't pass to his lungs. Normally we cough, but he can't right now. Joel is doing the job of the respirator by squeezing that green bag he attached to Nathan's mouth tube."

The second nurse slid a long tube into the mouth piece, clearing it of bubbles. Seventy, eighty, ninety. The monitor relaxed and quit its alarm. Joel reconnected the respirator hose to Nathan. Its piercing alarm hushed.

Matt's eyes burned, but he couldn't even blink.

Nancy looked at him twice. "We can go to the waiting room if you like, Matt."

Startled from his frozen state, Matt shook his head. He couldn't leave Nathan yet. It didn't take a genius to know twelve pieces of equipment keeping Nathan alive meant he may never have another visit. No matter how sick he felt, he had to stay.

Nancy left and Chuck visited. Gratefully, Matt sat down on the stool that Joel rolled to the head of Nathan's bed. Last Wednesday, laughing at the squirrel in the octopus tree had been normal. Now, everything buzzed abnormal. By lunchtime, with a stomach in a hundred knots, eating was not an option.

A doctor reviewed Nathan's chart and monitors with Joel. "Let's try another unit of Fresh Frozen." He lifted the sheet and checked large bandages on both leg stumps.

Having ignored the unusual short outline of Nathan's legs under the sheet, gruesome reality rushed at Matt.

"Good afternoon. I'm Dr. Farley. Are you Nathan's brother?"

"Best friend. I'm Matt."

"Well, Matt, you can see Nathan is very sick. But if it wasn't for wearing his bicycle helmet, he wouldn't have stood a chance."

"Then why doesn't he wake up?"

"He's had a lot of injury to his heart and lungs. His body wanted to work harder than the machines and it made the injuries worse. He's in a coma because of medication we give him to allow his body time to heal."

"How will you know when it's healed?"

"The machines won't work as hard."

"Why was the other leg taken off? Only one was under the train."

"You saw that leg?" Acknowledging Matt's nod, the doctor explained. "Although the other leg was attached, it was too damaged to ever have proper blood flow. I'm sorry we couldn't save his legs. There'll be tough days ahead for Nathan as he learns to walk with artificial legs. He'll be able to do all he did before, just differently. You'll both need to remember that."

"Can he hear us?"

"He's receiving large doses of pain medication, so I doubt he's conscious. If he has a good night, we'll let him wake up tomorrow." Dr. Farley nodded and walked to the next bed.

An invisible weight pressed down on Matt's chest. What if he, Matt, woke up tomorrow morning and was told he didn't have his legs anymore?

Joel put a hand on Matt's shoulder. "Are you all right?"

Ever since the phone call that first night, Matt knew in his head life had changed. This morning, intense loss broke his heart into pieces. His vision blurred and his chest shuddered a sob. Tears poured from his eyes. He clutched the wad of tissues Joel pressed into his hand and let them soak up memories of walking to school, running, biking, and climbing the octopus tree.

IN SPITE OF the late afternoon sun warming the truck's interior, Matt shivered. "Thanks for taking me in, Chuck. I know my dad had things to do for the campaign."

"You're welcome. I wanted to ask you another favour. Nathan's pup is a handful right now. Nancy hasn't left the hospital and my parents are in their eighties. Would you take Turbo for a few weeks until Nathan's out of the hospital—if your parents agree?"

"Sure. I'll take him home now. They won't mind."

"Your dad phoned and asked if you'd remind your Uncle Ted today of the photo session at your house on Tuesday. You're helping him with the campaign?"

"Whenever I can. I don't want him to get depression again."

"He's done well for a year."

He had. Matt always did his best to please his dad. "I want to keep it that way."

When they pulled in the driveway, Sarah sat on the front steps. Turbo, now seven pounds and three months old, wagged his tail so hard that his hips swung like a pendulum. Matt scooped him into his arms and sunk his face into the soft blond fur. Turbo squirmed excitedly. Today, no one mentioned the rule of "no licking faces."

Sarah held the door open for them. "Come on," she said to Matt. "I'll help collect his toys from Nathan's room."

A familiar voice boomed, "Matt! Nice to see you."

Matt held out his hand. "Hi, Grandpa Nadeau." Today, the elderly man's broad smile drooped. Turbo sneaked in another lick.

Grandpa rubbed Turbo's ears. "I'm getting too old for a young pup."

"I'm taking him home for a while. Nathan's pretty sick. Have you seen him?"

"Yes, I have."

"No one says it, but he could die."

"I'm praying day and night that God wants him here more than in heaven." As Turbo squirmed in Matt's arms, Grandpa Nadeau smiled. "You two better pack up the renegade."

They gathered the toys spread across the floor of Nathan's bedroom. Sarah handed Matt his camera. "I want to show you something," she whispered.

Matt unfolded the orange paper she handed him. NO BIKE-A-THON WANTED.

Puzzled, he read it twice. "Where did this come from?"

"On a tree where the bike trail begins. Nathan found it the day before the accident. My parents are going to ask you to take over the bike-a-thon. I thought you should know."

"Your dad asked me this morning."

"Will you do it?"

"I don't know yet. Organizing something this big and giving a speech is impossible for someone like me."

"Nathan started to put some stuff on his computer. It might help."

Matt tucked the note into a pocket. "I'll come tomorrow after church and take a look. Thanks." He clipped the leash to Turbo's collar, said good-bye to everyone, and wondered about the note as he walked to his uncle's house one street over.

Uncle Ted stood at the kitchen counter crushing pop cans in his homemade can crusher. "Hey, Matt, how's it going? Any word on Nathan?"

"I saw him this morning." He set Turbo down, who immediately sniffed a bag of pop cans. "He's pretty sick. I'm looking after Turbo until he's better." While Uncle Ted fed the machine, Matt told him about the morning visit.

Matt's thirteen-year-old cousin, Allie, sauntered into the kitchen. She stopped at the sight of him. Matt, as surprised to see her in a housecoat with her hair wrapped in a towel, smothered a laugh. Who had a shower at four o'clock in the afternoon? Then he noticed her red nose and watery eyes. "Got a cold?" he asked.

Allie furrowed her eyebrows in suspicion. "What are you doing here?"

Uncle Ted glared at her and crushed more cans. "Matt, I'll have about four bags of crushed cans for Nathan. They'll be worth about thirty dollars."

Allie rolled her eyes. "There won't be a bike-a-thon now, Dad."

"Don't count on it. It's for a good cause. You should ride in it."

Allie turned around. "I'm babysitting that day." And she coughed her way to the other side of the house.

By the time Matt walked home, it had been hours since he'd eaten. The spicy fragrance of sloppy-joes in the kitchen set his stomach rumbling. "I'm home, Mom!"

"Be up in five minutes."

With Turbo under one arm, he headed to his room and flopped onto the floor.

Turbo tripped over Matt's legs in his excitement to explore the room. With front paws against the bottom drawer of the dresser, the puppy peered inside it. Matt reached for the camcorder and clicked it on as Turbo worked hard to climb in. Finally, his back leg caught the drawer's edge and he plopped inside, out of sight. Then, like a submarine telescope, his head popped up and he yipped before disappearing again.

Matt hit the off button and laughed the first time in three days.

Turbo scurried along the drawer and found the leather glove Matt had picked up in the alley. He shook it in his mouth, his hips moving in circles, growling at the leather. Within a minute, he'd curled up on it and slept.

Matt slipped downstairs. He devoured three sloppy-joes. While deciding whether or not to have a fourth, the doorbell rang. Mom stood up. "There's coffee made, Tim. I have laundry to finish and I can't put it off another day." She escaped downstairs.

Matt raced to the door ahead of Dad to let Chuck in. Instead, two police officers stood on the porch. Matt recognized Officer Mary from the accident.

"Mr. Timmotay," the large male officer said, "we'd like to ask Matthew a few questions pertaining to the accident. Could we come in for a few minutes?"

"Certainly."

Matt followed them to the living room. A tingle slid along his spine. Now where did that come from and why?

Officer Ray introduced himself while Officer Mary flipped open her notepad. "Matthew," he asked, "were you and Nathan together prior to the accident last Wednesday?"

"Sort of." All eyebrows rose, especially his father's. Matt added, "We'd been together. Then we separated for about ten minutes, planning to meet at the tracks."

"What were you doing before the accident when you were together?"

"We were taking photos in the park for the bike-a-thon to go with Nathan's speech."

"That's where you separated?"

He decided "almost" would raise eyebrows as much as "sort of" so he dodged the question. "Sarah, Nathan's sister, was posing for the photo."

Officer Mary scribbled on her notepad. Her partner continued, "A call came in about ten minutes before the accident from Tom's Donut Shop about kids doing graffiti."

Matt schooled emotion from his face. A cool wind breezed in, almost as if Ball Cap was breathing down his neck.

"Were you one of those kids, Matthew?"

Him? Matt's throat tightened. "No. I wouldn't do that to Tom."

"Can you explain how your fingerprints came to be on one of the paint cans?"

Dad gasped, eyes darting between Officers Ray and Mary. Matt's skin shrivelled into tight goose bumps. He desperately wanted to protect his father, but if Ball Cap found out Matt had squealed on them, Ball Cap's revenge would be swift. "It must be a mistake."

Dad's voice tightened. "Matt, what's going on?"

Officer Ray's eyes steadied on Matt. "The prints matched yours taken at the school in the child protection program. Tom swears you weren't one of the three he saw. Did you supply the paint?"

"No."

"Have any of those three threatened you?"

Hypothetically, they would.

Officer Mary spoke for the first time. "Can you tell us anything?"

Matt shook his head and looked away. Officer Ray reminded him graffiti was against the law. "If you're involved in this, it's best we know now."

Silence.

The officers prepared to leave and Dad walked them to the door. Matt closed his eyes, aware of their muffled voices. Ball Cap and his thugs had already turned life upside down this week to the point of life and death. Now the police walked a graffiti trail past the guilty and straight to Matt. If anyone needed a miracle, he did.

God, if you let Nathan live—if you keep Dad from getting depression over these fingerprints . . . make them disappear or something—then I'll do the bike-a-thon for Nathan. I'll give it my best.
I know it's a bargain, but he's my very best friend. It'll take a miracle, but doing miracles is your business. Right?   Amen.

Dad stepped into the living room. Upstairs, a shrill scream ripped through the silence.

CHAPTER 3

THE LAUNDRY! Matt raced up the stairs behind his father. He peered over Dad's left shoulder. Mom knelt on the floor, fending off Turbo's darting tongue each time he hurtled at her. "I dropped your socks into the drawer and it came alive. I thought he was a wild rodent."

Visions of calm, disciplined Mom actually stamping her feet and screaming splintered Matt's anxiety. Smothering a laugh, he sucked in a shaky breath, but when Mom chortled, he did too. "Is it okay for him to stay here a few weeks? Nathan's family aren't coping with him right now."

"Of course, Matt." Mom stood up and hung a shirt in his closet. "Perhaps in the future you could give me notice so that I'm less overwhelmed by the unexpected."

Matt cringed.

Already, his father's dull eyes stared at the wall. That fast, the greying man had slipped into his own private world.

"Who was downstairs?"

Dad repeated every detail, almost word for word. When he finished, Mom sucked in a deep breath. She claimed it helped to file information in her brain. Today, the filing was short because Mom fired questions at him without waiting for answers. "Have you picked up a paint can someone dropped near the Donut Shop? Have you touched any paint cans this week? Have you been painting at school or with Nathan for the bike-a-thon?"

Yes. Yes. No. Simple enough to explain, except the police would consider him a witness. They would claim his video for evidence. Since Ball Cap didn't exactly fit America's Most Wanted, they'd leave him to fend for himself. As much as he hated doing this to his parents, it would blow over in a week or two and be forgotten.

Convinced of that, Matt went to bed early and slept. Near midnight, intense lightning illuminated his room and he shielded his eyes. Rain battered his window. When the sky rumbled above the house, Turbo pawed the bed and whined. Matt lifted the trembling pup into his arms. "Sh-h-h." Burrowing under the blankets, Turbo nestled against his thigh where he slept until Sunday dawned warm and sunny.

Although the phone had been silent in the night, Matt checked the answering machine straight away. No messages. Good, Nathan was still alive.

At church, the minister gave thanks that Nathan had survived four days and he prayed for his full recovery. Matt squeezed his eyes tight with determination. He confirmed his own deal with God. He'd keep his end of the pact. Not even Ball Cap would stop him.

Matt gulped down a glass of milk with his lunch and hurried to Nathan's house. Opening the door, Sarah embraced an excited Turbo. Her blond ponytail swung back and forth as she dodged high-speed licks. "We're in the kitchen. Come on."

Matt removed the leash and followed her. "It smells wonderful in here. Are you finished with lunch?"

Grandma Nadeau pointed to Nathan's empty chair at the table. "Have a piece of lemon cake. Might as well eat Nathan's portion until he can. That won't be long, because he's had a good twenty-four hours. The doctors are very pleased this morning." Grandpa Nadeau's wrinkles moved into a big smile.

Turbo searched for his food dish and settled for a dog biscuit instead. Grandpa Nadeau nodded to the pup. "Settling in okay, is he?"

"Fine. He's taken a liking to my dresser's bottom drawer."

"Always likes to climb into things or under them."

"I've thought about the bike-a-thon for Nathan. I've decided to do it."

Grandpa Nadeau murmured, "Nice. That's the second-best news I've heard today. We'll tell Chuck as soon as we see him."

"Thank you for the cake. I'd better check Nathan's computer for the bike-a-thon and see what's on my agenda first."

Sarah followed him to Nathan's room. "I'll open it for you," she offered. "We're going to the hospital this afternoon. You can lock up when you leave. So, what happened when you and Nathan left the park? Obviously, you caught up with the thief."

Alarms rang in Matt's head. He had forgotten what Sarah knew. "Have the police been here?"

"A few times."

Startled that she may have shared more with the police than he had, apprehension shuddered through him. "Sarah, did you tell them we chased that guy?"

"No. They just asked if we'd been taking pictures in the park. Why?"

Matt leaned against the desk, breathing easier. "The guy stopped in an alley and got off the bike. So, we took it. Look, Sarah, there's others involved. Don't say anything."

"The bike belonged to Nathan!"

"Sh-h-h."

Sarah dropped her voice. "It's okay. They're mostly deaf." She clicked the mouse. "Here's his stuff." They switched places at the computer and Matt scrolled down the screen. Sarah hesitated a moment, biting a fingernail, then asked, "How bad does he look? Will I faint?"

In a rush of sympathy for Sarah, Matt tried smiling and knew it wobbled. He wanted to tell her the smells almost made you faint and seeing Nathan made you cry. Instead, he said, "There are tubes and machines everywhere. The room constantly beeps, rings, and hisses.

The ends of his legs are bandaged and under a sheet. If you feel faint, take some deep breaths. It helps."

"Thanks. See you at school tomorrow."

While Matt put paper in the printer, the front door clicked and the house silenced. If he concentrated hard enough, he could forget about the hospital for a while.

Turbo's patter on the floor faded towards the kitchen, but he returned to report someone had definitely stolen his food dish. Matt dropped a biscuit to him as the computer screen exploded with colourful outlines for the bike-a-thon. Nathan's organization deserved top marks. Remembering how often he'd squabbled with Nathan that he used unnecessary energy to get the same results, Nathan's efforts had clearly made this project easier for someone else to complete. "Thank you, Nathan."

He hit print, scrolled down and whistled. "Oh wow, here's his speech."

Half the battle of a speech, especially for someone who struggled with words, was writing one. What a perfect last resort, should he need it. He could ask Mrs. Bailey if he could do it last, in light of the circumstances, and use it as his own. Adding a page to raise extra money for the legs should be easy enough.

That idea germinated all the while he tapped onto the internet, searching for childhood amputations. A web site names CHAMPS popped up and detailed an assortment of artificial limbs. Swimming legs drained water and prevented rust. Since a reference to biking legs wouldn't open, he sent off a short email requesting information specific to them.

"Turbo, we can do this. When Nathan wakes up, he'll know the bike-a-thon is on." Turbo's ears perked up.

BY THE TIME they arrived home with copies of ads and the speech, the sun had dried most of the pavement. In his bedroom, Matt slipped pen and paper into his back pocket, then he skipped downstairs. He poked his head into the living room. "I'm going to the park to count how many signs I need for the bike-a-thon. Turbo's had a good run and is asleep in the drawer. Need anything on the way home?"

Mom sat on the sofa with feet tucked up beside her, holding a can of furniture polish on her lap. Mom always dusted when upset, but Matt couldn't smell the polish. Dad stared at the dark fireplace. Both parents shook their heads. Responsibility stabbed Matt's conscience.

Maybe, he thought, setting out on his bicycle, he could swear his parents to secrecy. So what if they knew he feared Ball Cap? Then he remembered the fight with Tim Baldwin in Grade Two. Dad invited the Baldwin family on a picnic so Matt and Tim could become friends. He certainly didn't want Ball Cap at Sunday dinner.

At the tracks, Matt pushed away visions of Nathan's bloody leg. Before crossing over, he looked each way three times. Across from Tom's Donuts, he eased up on the pedals. In his mind, the alley moaned with the greatest injuries because it started here. It tightened the knot in his stomach. Never again would he enter that alley.

"Hey, Matt."

Matt had stayed home from school the rest of the week, so he hadn't seen any classmates since the accident. Jeremy Tooley and John Lees ran over to him. "We heard Nathan died," said Jeremy. "Is it true?"

Matt scowled. "No. I saw him yesterday. He's very sick, but he's alive." Indignant that anyone would say someone was dead when they weren't, Matt refused to add that it took twelve pieces of equipment to keep him that way.

John glanced towards the park and Matt followed his gaze. "Too bad about the bike-a-thon. I don't like begging for money anyway."

Sighting Ball Cap sitting on a bench in the park, Matt ignored his racing heart. "I'm taking it over for Nathan. It's for a good cause, guys. And Nathan needs legs for swimming and biking. Maybe we can raise extra money for them."

"What?" sputtered John. "Do you know how much money that'll take?"

"Not yet, but I'm looking into it."

Jeremy followed Matt's gaze to the park and said, "The project's too big for Grades Five and Six. Maybe Junior High would join us." He nodded towards Ball Cap. "Give him something to do besides beat up people." Jeremy cupped his hands around his mouth and yelled,

"Hey Ball Cap, beat up all your friends? You look a little lonely."

Jeremy and John bid Matt farewell and sprinted away. Ball Cap stood up and shuffled to the gate. Great. Judging the distance between himself and Ball Cap, Matt almost rode away with the others, but he hesitated. After all, Ball Cap stood alone.

"Hey, Timmotay!"

Matt used his most boring voice. "Yeah?"

Ball Cap stopped six feet away with hands shoved deep in the pockets of oversize denims. "My buddy wasn't too happy about his bike being stolen like that the other evening."

A flash of Nathan hooked to machines flitted across Matt's mind. "You tell your friend I wasn't too happy my friend got hurt taking back his own bike." Hardly believing those words had come out of his own mouth, Matt clamped his lips together.

Ball Cap's small eyes shifted. "He wasn't anywhere near those tracks. You better not repeat that allegation to the police."

Unsure what "allegation" meant, Matt forced calm into his voice. "The police have their own worries with accidents and graffiti around town. I doubt they care what I think."

Ball Cap's eyes narrowed in his square face. Recognizing silence as an opportunity to escape with his pride intact, Matt nodded. "See ya." He pedaled directly across the street, pleased with himself.

When Ball Cap disappeared one block away, Matt spun around and rode to the park. Always upon entering the park, Nathan and he would search the octopus tree for a particular brown squirrel. Whoever saw it first whistled at it. Today, the squirrel busied itself with something it held. Out of habit, Matt whistled. The squirrel jumped to attention.

Reaching the bicycle trail's entrance, Matt searched the town's BONESHAKER TRAIL sign. Finding another note would have made Ball Cap the prime suspect since he'd been here moments ago, but the sign stood clean.

Nathan had discovered the slang name, boneshaker, given to history's early bicycles because their solid wheels had given a rough ride. Further in on this trail, two metal grid bridges crossed over the ravine's shallow creek. Vibrations from the grids imitated those first bicycles. Immediately, Town Council had welcomed Boneshaker Trail.

Engrossed in that part of Nathan's speech, Matt pedaled a half kilometre on the path before the present caught up with him. Far ahead, a bare maple tree, not yet sprouting spring foliage, sported bold orange paper. The paper's edge flickered in the breeze.

Matt strained his ears for sounds other than his own bicycle and heard only the wind. Some distance to his right, he studied a dilapidated hut down by an abandoned bridge where the old road used to weave around the park. It was without any sign of human life, and he glanced over his shoulder. The empty trail satisfied him. So, how did one piece of orange paper have its own presence?

The bicycle lurched. Matt clenched the handlebars in a desperate attempt to hold on, but his body hurtled forward, ripping the bars out of his hands. He flew right over the bicycle. In midair, he tried to push his arms out to break the fall, but he hit the ground quicker. Pain shot through his chest. The landing whipped his head back and forward against the hard ground. He lay there with his face against the ground, the smell of dirt filling his nostrils.

He sucked in a painful breath and eased his body to a sitting position. As he wiped dirt from his mouth, blood poured from his chin.

Matt kicked off a running shoe. He rolled a sock into a ball and held it in place. The breeze blew colder. He shivered in the silent bush.

Once he caught his breath, he walked to the tree and ripped off the damp paper. LAST WARNING. NO BIKES WANTED.

In spite of a throbbing chin, Matt kicked the leaves away from behind his bicycle. He scowled at the shallow trench.

Half an hour later, his parents whisked him to the Emergency department where they glued him back together again, literally. "It's skin glue," the doctor smiled. "Less scarring. And you won't have to come back." He handed Matt a mirror.

Mom beamed at the tidy glue job. "What'll they think of next?"

The doctor shone a light in his eyes, searched his ears, and probed his jaw. "It looks like you're okay. No concussion."

"I had my helmet on."

"Good. Keeps your brain from turning into mush."

"You must all learn that at medical school. The doctor in Critical Care said the same thing about my friend there."

"We do learn it at school. Then we see it first-hand in the hospitals." The doctor sent them on their way. "And fix that hole on the trail."

Matt led the way to the elevators. "It's a funny hospital. We take the elevator down to the second floor. Nathan might be waking up today."

Mom and Dad followed. When they rounded the corner, the center elevator stood open. Matt halted in his tracks. Ball Cap trailed behind a heavily bearded man. The elevator doors closed as he turned around inside it.

Confused and relieved, Matt watched the light move up to higher floors. Running into Ball Cap twice in one day would put anyone on high alert.

Nancy sprung from her chair in the packed waiting room, held Matt's head between two hands, and scrutinized his injury. "What happened?"

When all eyes in the room descended upon Matt, he cringed with embarrassment. "I'm fine. I fell off my bike. We can't stay long so I better go in."

As Matt ducked out the door, Nancy's arms swept around each of his parents. Matt talked stiffly into the intercom. Julie, the Charge Nurse, kept a watchful eye on Nathan while Joel took his break. She sat at the end of the bed, preparing a syringe. "He's been awake a few times this morning."

"Does he know about his legs?"

"Yes. His parents told him about an hour ago."

Nathan knew. Worried, Matt slid his hands into his pockets. If Nathan woke up now, what could he say to him?

"How was he when they told him?"

"Very upset. It'll take a few days—oh look, I think he's waking up again."

Matt stepped to Nathan's head and smiled nervously. "Hi Nathan."

Nathan lifted his hand an inch off the mattress and waved his fingers.

Julie explained, "He can't talk until we take him off the respirator. Nathan, do you want the board to write on?"

He held out a hand. His eyes shifted in different directions without moving his head. In similar circumstances, Matt knew he'd move as little as possible, but it made handwriting difficult to read.

I DON'T HAVE LEGS.

A flash of Nathan's leg under the train shot through Matt's memory. Matt whispered, "I know."

Nathan scribbled again. WHERE ARE THEY?

"Where are your legs?"

Nathan pointed a finger to the end of the bed, and Matt followed its direction to Julie.

She slid off her stool and came closer. "No one's ever asked me that. I'll have to find out for you, Nathan. Is it really important you know this?"

He nodded.

"Okay, give me a day to find out. I'm on tomorrow."

Nathan closed his eyes a moment, then scribbled on the board again. Matt reached for the eraser and cleaned the board's lower end while Julie rolled a stool towards him. Matt studied the scribble. Nathan wrote it again.

Joel returned and he scanned the board too. "Bike? Something about a bike?"

"The bike-a-thon?" asked Matt.

Nathan nodded, setting off a spasm of coughing that triggered the respirator's alarm. Joel's hand spread across Nathan's chest. "It's a reflex. Relax. Breathe in, breathe out. What were you saying, Matt, about a bike-a-thon?"

Concentrating hard, Matt breathed in, breathed out.

Joel silenced the piercing alarm beside the bed. Two beds over, alarms blared one after another. Joel pulled the curtain to the foot of Nathan's bed. "Go ahead, Matt," said Joel, and he nodded his head.

Matt breathed in. "The bike-a-thon is on. With Sarah's help, I found the ads on your computer. We're going to do it."

Drawing a smiley face on the board, Nathan closed his eyes. The marker slipped from his hand.

"It's impossible for him to stay awake long," explained Joel. "You came in at the perfect time. He'll sleep an hour or two now."

"I'd better go. My parents are waiting for me. When he wakes up, tell him I'll be back soon."

In spite of the short visit, Matt's mood soared with energy and hope. Then they turned onto their street. In front of their house, Officers Ray and Mary waited in their cruiser.

Matt's optimism plunged into a nose dive.

As soon as everyone sat in the living room, Officer Ray declared the fingerprints to be incriminating evidence. Matt, stiff with fear, listened to five people breathing. The officer fixed his eyes upon him. "Nathan reported his new silver bicycle stolen a week prior to the accident, yet Nathan rode that bicycle when the accident occurred. Can you explain that, Matthew?"

Matt stared at Officer Ray. Without warning, his throat convulsed under the stares of Dad, Mom, and Officer Mary. In spite of the room's lemon fresh sparkle, the air hung thick and stuffy.

Instead of blowing over, this situation had jumped from bad to worse.

Chapter 4

The living room plunged into silence. In the kitchen across the hall, Turbo lapped water.

"We saw Nathan's bike in the alley," said Matt. "So we took it." Not exactly the whole truth, but it worked.

Constable Mary's pen hovered over her notebook. "You knew for certain it was Nathan's bicycle?"

"Sure."

Turbo padded into the living room. When he saw Matt, his tail broke into a gusty wag and he sprinted towards him. Matt lifted the pup onto his lap. He fired off a silent S.O.S. call like the minister preached about on Sunday.

Officer Ray asked, "Why didn't you mention this the other day?"

"You asked where we were before the accident. We were in the park. Spotting Nathan's bike just happened." Matt forced his eyes up.

Officer Ray never blinked. "And the fingerprints?"

Everything came back to the fingerprints. "It's all I know. I'm sorry. I wish I could help you." His breathing, shallow and tight, stayed that way until the officers left. He closed his eyes, wondering why he ever thought he could outwit the police in the first place.

Matt stayed home from school Monday because Mom shone a flashlight into his eyes every three hours after the accident and she had the same plan for the day. "Aunt Mary always said twenty-four hours after a bump on the head could show a concussion, and she was a nurse."

"Yes, but Aunt Mary was a hundred years old. Technology advanced."

"Technology, yes, but the human brain has been consistently the same. Aunt Mary was only ninety-eight, so don't exaggerate."

That meant, "don't argue." And he didn't, but on Tuesday morning Matt dressed early and ran out the door before Mom could protest. Dark gray clouds hung low over the town. A cold wind whipped his collar and he stopped by the park to zip his jacket.

In the distance down the bike trail, the Township fed small tree branches into a mulch machine. Like Uncle Ted's can crusher, they went in one way and came out another.

The Nadeau's black pick-up truck drew alongside the curb. Sarah jumped out the passenger door, disappearing in a cloud of thick white exhaust. Mornings were still cold in April.

Chuck leaned out the driver's window. "Matt, I'm going to see Nathan this evening after supper. Want to come along? He has a surprise for you."

A surprise? Immediately, legs flashed across Matt's mind, but he gave himself a mental shake. Legs didn't grow back. "Thanks. I will."

"See you around six-thirty," Chuck said as he sped off.

Sarah walked with Matt to school. "Nathan's face is different."

"A nurse said big injuries do that, and so do drugs that decrease the swelling in his brain. I hardly recognized him the first time."

"I didn't faint."

"Good."

"There's so many sick kids."

"Really sick. Makes organizing a bike-a-thon look like a small thing."

"It's big to Nathan. You're still doing it, aren't you? What happened to your chin?"

Because Sarah had confided in him about the note, he told her about the trench. Sarah's blue eyes darkened under eyebrows pulled tight together. Matt shrugged. "So, now we have two warnings. Both on orange paper."

"Someone really doesn't want that Ride to happen. I wonder who?"

"Wish I knew." Matt heard a call and searched the students ahead. "There's Abby. Don't tell anyone, Sarah. If our parents find out, they'll never let us do the ride."

Sarah agreed and ran off to join her friend.

Mrs. Bailey's English class was first on Tuesdays. The last thing he wanted to face was an inquiry on how dead Nathan looked, so he busied himself at his locker until one minute before the bell. When Matt walked into the silent classroom, he slowed down. Mrs. Bailey stood beside Jeremy Miller's desk, her right hand on her hip, her left hand stretched open in front of his chest. Jeremy placed a whistle on her palm and slouched down in his seat.

Mrs. Bailey slipped the whistle into her pocket and smiled at Matt as if she had eyes in the back of her head and knew he'd arrived. "Nice to see you back, Matt."

"Thank you, Mrs. Bailey."

"Mr. Nadeau told me Nathan's improving." Murmurs rose around the room. "Mr. Nadeau also had good news about the bike-a-thon. Matt?"

When Mrs. Bailey motioned him to the front of the classroom, he wished he'd stayed home with Mom's flashlight. Looking at his classmates, Matt determined to keep his end of the bargain. He could do this.

"We … all know," he began, frantically searching for the words that Chuck had used on him, "about Nathan's passion to raise money for the playground equipment. So, I'm organizing the bike-a-thon for him." A few claps arose. "Nathan will need swimming and biking legs. Extra money we raise would help those expenses."

Martha Brown waved her hand in the air, a ring on every finger and thumb. "We could get the whole school to help."

Jeremy shook his head and sighed loudly. "Nathan might be doing better, but he's still on the critical list and could die. It's a lot of work for someone who might never know we did it for him."

Murmurs grew in agreement and disagreement. Martha Brown excitedly prepped her group of classmates for a yes vote. Matt looked at Jeremy. "Nathan's going to live."

The room hushed.

Jeremy, slouched, stared at him with eyebrows raised high on his forehead. "You don't know that."

All eyes turned on Matt. Confident, he replied, "Yes, I do know. Besides, the kids need the equipment as much this week as they did last week before Nathan got hurt. I hope we'll give it our best shot, for Nathan AND for the kids." Matt returned to his desk. Martha's side of the room murmured agreement.

By the time he arrived home from school, Mom had put away her flashlight. She met him at the front door waving a twenty dollar bill at him. "You have an appointment at the barber's in ten minutes. The photo shoot, remember?"

"I remember." He slid his backpack across the floor to the bottom of the stairs. Turbo ran into the hall from the kitchen, carrying the leather glove like a favourite toy. His feet slid out from under him, his chin hit the floor, but he never lost his grip on the glove.

After the barber, Matt threw the ball for Turbo outside while the photographer set up his equipment.

Uncle Ted's car pulled into the driveway. Matt knew he'd been to Aunt Kay's hairdresser because the gray was gone. Allie rolled out of the car and slammed the door shut. Spiked hair glowed brilliant fluorescent pink.

Dumbfounded, Matt watched her procession up the sidewalk. Aunt Kay looked nervously between Allie and Matt's dad. "Tim, you're a politician who represents all walks of life, aren't you?"

Dad blinked, couldn't quite find his voice, and then actually laughed. "Yes, all walks of life. Allie! I'm glad you came."

Allie softened a little, even cracked a tiny smile before she kissed Matt's dad on his cheek. "Will we be done in half an hour? I'm meeting friends."

Uncle Ted spoke quietly. "I told you you're staying with us for supper."

"I told you I'm not." She stomped to the living room and flopped onto the sofa.

Everyone looked at each other before they followed.

The photographer called for Matt's attention twice. Matt forced a smile, preoccupied with pink hair and a dark alley one week ago. Although Allie had changed a lot in the past year, it didn't mean the villains had claimed her. Did it?

Turbo chose that moment to make a grand entrance, the leather glove in his mouth as he straddled it between his four legs. He plunked down by the tripod, frog-style.

The photographer sucked in his breath. "A puppy! Perfect!" He scooped up Turbo, ignored the fallen glove, and placed the pup in Dad's arms. As soon as the camera clicked, Matt studied Allie's hair yet again. Surely it dazzled more than the other girl's hair.

Allie stared at the glove, chewing her bottom lip.

Pink Hair had danced around the alley when she hurt her hand. Cringing, Matt spotted the band aid on Allie's left index finger. An ice-cube inched down his neck.

Dad convinced Allie to stay for dinner. The aroma of garlic bread probably helped his case. "We've cooked your favourite meal—spaghetti—and we have Gram's sauce."

"You're thoughtful, Uncle Tim. My parents ate the last jar we had when I wasn't home."

Aunt Kay gasped through strained lips. "You never told us it was your favourite."

"Right," Allie drawled. "Most parents know their kid's favourite foods."

If Allie had wanted a reaction from both parents, she certainly got one. Matt slipped out of the room. Upstairs, he closed his bedroom door and took the video camera from his bedside table. He held the rewind button until the dark alley showed on screen. He pressed play.

Ball Cap and his buddy looked full face to the camera several times, but Pink Hair never did. It didn't matter. He knew.

"Matt!" Dad called from downstairs. "Supper's ready."

"Coming." He set the camera back into its case, set it on the floor of his closet and covered it with dirty clothes.

Allie would never have reason to come upstairs, but it didn't hurt to be cautious. Pink Hair was in the house.

That evening at the hospital, Mr. and Mrs. Nadeau had errands to run, so Matt entered the Critical Care Unit by himself. A plastic green mask, like the one he'd worn at the accident, covered Nathan's face. Excitement exploded like a celebration of firecrackers. "He's off the respirator."

Joel grinned. "I took two days off and look at his progress."

Matt walked to the head of the bed. Someone had washed his hair. "Can you talk?"

"Finally," he croaked. "They took the tube out this morning. My voice will be back to normal in a day or two."

Pushing away regret that Nathan's legs wouldn't ever be back to normal, Matt counted the equipment. Five. Two chest tubes remained. "Do you hurt anywhere?"

"Not bad. I feel my feet, but when I try to wiggle my toes, only my knees move." He did it to prove his point.

Because of Nathan's sincerity, Matt searched Joel's face. "He can feel his toes?"

"It's called phantom pain and it's quite normal after an amputation to feel pain or cold in the missing limb. It'll lessen with exercise and with time as the brain conditions itself to the new situation."

"I'm not hallucinating," added Nathan. "Tell him about the chair."

"It's like sitting in a chair you've sat in a million times only you miss the seat because someone moved it a few feet over. Your brain needs to adjust to the change."

Clutching the stool with both hands, just in case, Matt sat close to the bed.

Nathan asked, "You know all the pictures you take?"

"Yes."

"I can't remember what my legs looked like. The doctor says they incinerate limbs. He said he wouldn't show them to me even if he had them."

A vision flashed of Nathan's legs tossed into an incinerator, shoes and all. Matt blinked hard, concentrating on Nathan's raspy voice.

"I can't remember what they looked like when they were on me. Can you?"

"I'm not sure. You always raved about your running shoes."

"Yeah, when I had feet to wear them. I want to see my legs. Will you look through your pictures and see if you can find close ups? My parents say they've looked and can't find any. I think they're just saying that."

"Okay, I'll look."

"Joel's going to take my stitches out. If he'll do it now, will you stay with me?"

Matt decided it was the hardest thing he'd ever had to do and he was never sure how he made it through that half hour. The skin stretched around the stumps of his legs so smoothly that he guessed they sanded the bone.

That gory image, mingled with odours of the bandages, rolled his stomach. He should have skipped supper.

Nathan lifted his head up from the pillow and watched Joel snip a knot. The first stitch tugged against the skin when Joel pulled the thread with tweezers. "Forceps," he corrected Matt's terminology.

Joel worked gently, and squirted salt water over the threads to loosen them. "Saline." One by one, the boys counted the stitches as Joel placed them on a disposable towel on Nathan's abdomen. "Sutures."

That night, Matt dreamed about forceps, scissors, sutures and saline. In the morning, he examined his chin in the bathroom mirror. The glue held. He gulped down an early breakfast and biked to Boneshaker Trail before school started.

The Township had repaired the trench just as Dad had said. He biked around the trail and counted sites for signs while wondering how many students would ride. At recess and lunch yesterday, classmates remained split on the project's value. Matt recalled more conversation about Nathan than the children of this project.

Because Nathan's speech focused on the children, it could encourage the most sceptical students to ride. That fact popped into his head over and over again. On the brighter side, his brain argued, flyers gave the same result.

Jeremy stood at Boneshaker's exit. "Hi there."

Matt braked. "Hi. What are you doing here so early?"

"I live across the street, remember? I saw you ride in here." He handed Matt an orange paper. "My dad's on the Township. They found this yesterday when clearing branches. It has your name on it."

Matt took the paper as if it might blow up. Scribbled across the top, he read his name. "Did you write this, Jeremy?"

"Not me, but someone's not happy about the bike-a-thon."

"You aren't."

Jeremy shrugged. "I'm not sure it's worth it. Twelve hundred dollars is a lot of money to raise, and what're you going to do if you don't make enough for the equipment? Why not have the whole school help instead of just grades five and six so you have a chance of raising the money? It's depressing for riders to fail in the end *and* go to a funeral."

In the cold morning air, Matt stared at the clouds above the octopus tree. All his life, he'd heard about Jesus' power on earth and from heaven. This morning, that power captured him. In spite of a horrific accident, Nathan lived. In spite of fingerprints and police, Dad lived free of depression. Today, with two miracles given to him just as he'd asked for, Matt breathed a deep thank you.

His purpose for the Ride shifted. More than proving Jeremy wrong, more than keeping his word to a bargain, he wanted to show his thanks to Jesus by passing on a miracle to those little children. No matter what, he'd do his best to make a successful bike-a-thon.

"You should go to the police about that note. My dad's worried someone will get hurt. Or tell your dad so that the Council can protect everyone."

Matt squashed Jeremy's theory for the Superheroes. "Come on, Jeremy. We better get to school."

Jeremy ran beside the bicycle. "Haven't you heard a word I've said?"

Chapter 5

Mrs. Bailey lingered in the classroom at the end of the day. Matt stood outside the door, glanced up and down the deserted hall, took a deep breath, and walked inside. "Mrs. Bailey, I've been thinking about the speech."

"Good. Have you reconsidered?"

"Yes, Mrs. Bailey."

She stopped sorting her papers. "I'm glad. What changed your mind?"

"I want the bike-a-thon to be successful and I want to be sure enough money is raised. I guess I have to do Nathan's rally idea, but because of the accident, could I do it last?"

"I could arrange that." She stapled a set of papers and set them aside. "I want you to remember something, Matt. I understand you want to do this for your best friend. The work involved in something this big and the respect of your peers is always important too. However, there will always be people who won't support you."

"You mean Jeremy?"

"There's nothing wrong with doing something for another and wanting to be successful at it, but your personal success is doing your best because it's deep in your heart to do it—not because you want to prove someone wrong."

It *was* deep in his heart . . . now. He nodded.

She studied her calendar and picked up a pencil. "Could you be ready by two weeks from Monday on May second?"

"Yes. Thank you, Mrs. Bailey."

Every night that week, Matt plugged away at writing the speech's end. Nathan grew stronger every day, and early in the week they transferred him to a regular floor. Matt snuggled into bed on Thursday night, dodging Turbo's licks. "He's tubeless, Turbo. Nathan is on his own power." Soon, he'd transfer to a special rehabilitation hospital where he'd learn to use artificial legs.

Friday afternoon, after Matt checked his email for a response to biking legs, he began memorizing the speech aloud in his room.

Dad poked his head through the doorway. "Matt, here's the photo papers. Are you sure you have time to deliver them house to house?" He set the box on his dresser.

"No problem. I'll start tomorrow."

"How's the speech going?"

"Slow."

After his father left, Matt stared at the box of five hundred papers. He promised to do this job two months ago when five hundred houses looked simple. Matt crunched his shoulders up and down, turning his head sideways. Dad depended on his help.

Much to Matt's surprise, Chuck stopped by in the afternoon to report Nathan had been transferred that day to the new hospital. "Nathan's brimming with doom and gloom. They're certain it's because he's coming off the steroids. He didn't even care that they measured him for his legs today. Do you think you can spend tomorrow afternoon with him, Matt?"

"Sure. Nathan can help me with my speech."

Mom spent the day helping Grandma Nadeau rearrange Nathan's room. She returned home with a bag of pop cans. "Grandpa Nadeau gave us these for Uncle Ted to crush for the bike-a-thon. Could you take it over after supper, Matt?"

"Sure. Turbo needs a good run."

By the time Matt finished his errands and climbed into bed that night, he had memorized one line of the speech.

The next afternoon, Matt stared up at Benson Rehabilitation Hospital. Before he reached the hospital's large double glass doors, they slid open automatically. As he stepped inside, a shiny purple scooter barrelled past him in the opposite direction. The driver, an old wiry man with white hair on the sides of a bald head, looked like he'd gotten lost in a time machine and ended up in modern time.

Seeing a door on his right marked SECURITY, Matt wondered if they gave drivers speeding tickets. He followed Chuck's directions to the fifth floor. When he found Nathan's room, he tiptoed in and peered around the curtain. Nathan waved, grim and silent.

That's how Dad acted when depressed. He'd lay in bed without any expression on his face. Already Matt knew anything he said would be ignored or argued. In spite of a familiar dread in his stomach, he smiled. "Hi Nathan. Nice room."

"It's okay."

He laid his backpack on the foot of the bed. "When do you get your legs?"

"I'm not like your chin. They can't glue me back together again."

"I meant your new legs. Who told you about my chin?"

"Sarah said you fell off your bike. I wish that's all that happened to me."

"Me too," agreed Matt.

Nathan sank further under the sheet. "I get my legs in a few days. What did you bring in the backpack?"

"Monopoly. And a speech."

"Is it speech time?"

"You don't remember writing a speech for the bike-a-thon?"

Nathan thought a moment. "No. I'm still having trouble remembering everything."

"That's okay. At least you remember the bike-a-thon."

Out in the hall, a whirling noise grew closer and louder. Next thing Matt knew, a familiar purple scooter swerved into the room and halted at the foot of Nathan's bed.

"Hello, boys," said the elderly gentleman with a strong French accent. He smiled as broad a smile as Grandpa Nadeau's. At the touch of a lever on the handle, the scooter sped forward to the other side of the room.

Nathan whispered, "There's no kids here. He's a likeable fellow."

Nathan found something to like about everyone. Except Ball Cap, of course.

Once the roommate parked his scooter, he walked back towards them. "I'm Frank." He shook Matt's hand. "You Nathan's brother?"

"Best friend. Nice to meet you. I like your wheels."

"Me too." Frank grinned. "I have a prosthetic leg myself—that's the politically correct word for artificial leg. At ninety years old, they've allowed me to drive again." His eyes shot to the scooter. "I told Nathan he can use it any time he wants."

"Really?" Matt exclaimed. Nathan stared at his bed sheets, wiggled his stumps, and clamped his mouth closed. Matt murmured, "Maybe when he's feeling better."

Frank agreed, but before he could say anything else, a staff nurse walked into the room. Her hair showed off at least fifty braids and her radiant smile revealed the whitest teeth. "Frank, you can't bring the scooter in here. Emergencies happen."

"I hope one does. Maybe I'll get some attention around here. I keep telling you, I need a check-up. They took blood from Nathan today and totally ignored me."

"You're in perfect health."

"You don't know that. Something could be brewing."

She disappeared behind the curtain and pulled it around his bed. "Come on. I'll put the news on before I move your scooter. I'll park it outside the door."

"Rules, rules, rules." He winked at Matt and Nathan and grinned for a split second.

He pulled his eyebrows down into a scowl before he disappeared behind the curtain too.

"Find any photos of my legs?"

"I'm still looking."

Nathan studied him.

"I am, really. I have three shoe boxes of photos and it takes time."

Nathan nodded. "Well, how about Monopoly? I think I remember how to play."

The low volume from Frank's television softened the room's silence. Nathan lasted long enough to buy three properties and two utilities before his heavy eyes shut a final time and he napped. Matt slipped the game into its box.

The nurse with braids came in with a can of pop for him. "It's been a big day for him. Want a tour of the floor?"

Felicia introduced herself as they left the room. She pointed to the kitchen and adjacent dining room. "Residents can find snacks and drinks here between their meals. We've had trouble nudging Nathan from his room. He's very self-conscious right now without legs."

If Nathan wouldn't leave his room, no wonder he didn't care about the scooter. "He's always worrying about his looks. Combs his hair every half hour."

"Come with me to the cafeteria. It's a safe place to start once he's willing to go off the floor. You'll be a big help in Nathan's recovery."

They rode the elevator to the basement, traveled down the long hall past the auditorium, wood working shop, and craft room and walked directly into the cafeteria.

"What are Nathan's hobbies?"

"Computers."

"We have a computer room. It's attached to the craft room. I'll show it to you on the way back."

Matt liked Felicia, who happened to like photography too. She promised to bring in photos of her family home in Africa.

That evening, no matter what he tried, Matt could not concentrate on his speech. Images of gloomy Nathan haunted him. Felicia called it grieving, only instead of losing a person, Nathan had lost his legs and their functions.

After church the next day, Matt lay on his bed with hands behind his head. He recited the speech's first paragraph and two sentences of the next. Nathan's tired face barged into his concentration again.

He rolled off his bed, searched through his closet, and pulled out a medium size duffle bag. After he packed a sweatshirt in the bottom, he carefully placed Turbo inside it. The puppy had lots of room. Small brown eyes looked up at Matt.

Convincing his parents he could safely ride his bicycle to the hospital proved impossible. "It's only thirty minutes away by car," he argued.

"Exactly," agreed Mom. "Recently, you were almost in a train accident with Nathan. You've gone over handlebars and had your chin glued together. I'll drive you."

"You don't trust me?"

"Right now, I don't trust the world. I'll be ready to leave in five minutes."

Matt fetched the duffle bag, tossed it onto the back seat of the car, and sat down in the front with Turbo on his lap.

Mom squinted her eyes. "Turbo's allowed?"

"It's a different kind of hospital, Mom. It's like a home away from home." He dodged the long pause on her side of the car by looking out the window, hoping she couldn't see his face. Mom set the car in drive.

At the front doors of the hospital, Matt waved to her until the car drove out of sight. With Turbo tucked under one arm, he hiked to a side entrance where a cluster of evergreen trees bordered the pavement. The shadows chilled the air on this side of the building. He stepped around the odd clump of snow near the lowest tree boughs. Watchful and nervous, he placed Turbo inside the bag. Lifting it carefully, his heart beating fast, he walked inside and traveled straight to Nathan's room.

With the curtain pushed back to the wall, warm spring sunshine flooded their room. Nathan slept. Frank snored.

Matt sat in the chair and slid open the bag's zipper. Turbo stretched a moment and yawned before Matt set him on the bed.

He uncapped the camcorder and focused on the reunion. Turbo's tail beat fiercely. He whined and snuggled up to Nathan frog-style. Nathan's sleepy eyes, dull for only a second, blazed with a brilliant light. He gasped. "Turbo!"

The pup washed every inch of his face, whined, rolled over, and crawled onto Nathan's chest. When he nestled against Nathan's neck, a burst of laughter touched the room.

Euphoria rushed through Matt's veins. The last time he'd heard that sound they were in a tree with a squirrel posing like Mrs. Bailey. He blinked hard. Pressing the zoom out button, the camcorder's field broadened and focused on Frank's watchful eyes. Matt's heart stopped.

Frank threw back the bed sheets, walked briskly to the door and closed it, then greeted Turbo as if he hadn't seen a real dog for decades. Turbo's tail never lost a beat and he washed Frank's face too.

Matt smiled at Nathan. "That dog is breaking all your father's rules."

Frank stared at Matt proudly. "How did you get him in here?"

"The side entrance. He loves to snuggle in things and sleeps every night with me under the blankets, so I put him in this duffle bag."

Frank sighed. "He is cute." Turbo stumbled over Frank's lap and lay across Nathan's chest. His tongue dangled and his teeth gleamed.

A rap on the door drew all eyes to the curtain's ripple at the end of the bed. With lightning reflexes, Frank scooped up Turbo. He lifted the sheet and set the puppy at Nathan's side. The sheet settled as Felicia stopped her water trolley. "Everything okay?"

"Fine," all three said at once.

Immediately, her eyebrows rose. "Did I interrupt something?"

Frank snorted. "No. Matt was videotaping, so I shut the door to keep the noise down. By the way, you haven't made my bed today."

Felicia's eyes danced. "You have to be out of it for it to be made. I'll be glad to do it.

Matt unclenched his teeth. Breathe in . Breathe out. He counted numbers in his head. She'd depart by the time he counted to twenty. One and two and three…

Having finished the bed, Felicia smiled. "Nathan, do you want some ice water?"

"Yes, please."

Ice cubes jangled from her pitcher into Nathan's jug. Turbo poked his head out from under the sheet. Nathan pushed him back. He lifted his knees to hide movement from Felicia, but four inches of leg below his knees made a small tent with the sheet.

Matt slipped the leather glove to Nathan who passed it to Turbo. He positioned the duffle bag at Nathan's knees to block Felicia's view of Turbo. Twelve and thirteen and fourteen…

When Felicia set the jug on the over-bed table, Nathan frowned. "Can you please put it on this end of the table?"

Felicia looked at him. Gently. Silently.

Matt slumped into his chair. He quit counting and he might as well quit breathing. These two squabbled over small details while an illegal puppy hid five feet away.

"Nathan, remember the exercises Physiotherapy taught you this week to build strength and to loosen your knees? Sitting up and reaching for the jug will extend your knees. It's a good exercise for you to do. I'd like you to keep the table here for an hour."

Nathan clamped his mouth into a tight line and scowled at the jug. Felicia waved goodbye. No one moved until the water trolley rolled out of the room.

The door clicked shut. As Turbo emerged from under the sheets, the door burst open.

Sarah whipped back the curtain. Perspiration dampened her bangs and her tangled ponytail bounced right over her shoulder. "Matt! The bike trail. It's in a terrible mess!"

Chapter 6

Later that day, Matt stood on the first bend of Boneshaker Trail. Empty pop cans, pop cans crushed in the middle, and pop cans crushed by Uncle Ted's can crusher littered the path. He'd know those cans anywhere.

Debris spread out at least a block long. Blue recycle bags wavered against tree trunks and bushes. With the sun setting and gray shadows on the trail growing longer, goose bumps tingled along Matt's arms. Gritting his teeth, he picked up a bag and crushed it into a ball. How could Allie do this to family?

Matt spun around and raced out of the park, past the road where he lived, and directly to Allie's house. When he burst into the kitchen through the back door, Allie froze in her steps. Her mouth dropped open for a second before she snapped, "Don't you ever knock?"

"What's your problem? Messing around with the bike trail, spreading cans all over it. Have you lost your mind?"

Allie rolled her eyes while twisting her mouth. "Funny how everyone asks me that lately. Forget how am I feeling, or how am I doing in school. Have I lost my mind?" She bit into her apple and threw the dishcloth towards the sink. It landed on the floor. She ignored it.

"What do you have against the bike-a-thon, Allie?"

"It's not going to happen. It's over."

"Why? What do you care if there's a bike-a-thon? You've already said you're babysitting."

Allie smiled. "I lied."

"You lied? Which part?"

"It's gotten complicated. I'm not surprised you can't figure it out." Allie held the apple between her teeth while she cracked the tab off a can of pop. "But I can't figure out something myself. My dad came home last evening after being with your dad and it seems you have fingerprints on a paint can connected to graffiti in town."

Matt objected to the way she twisted the conversation and reasoned, "You can't figure it out because you know I'm not part of the gang, but I know you couldn't get the lid off your paint can that night. You hurt your hand with the screwdriver, pulled off the glove, and that's the glove Turbo has."

Allie paled. She sipped her drink. "You must have been there. After all, the police have your fingerprints and you have one of our gloves."

"Why are you involved with these two? Ball Cap is trouble."

"Ball Cap?" she echoed, smothering a laugh. "We have a real leader. He's the one you better watch." Allie sat in the nearest chair and plunked down her pop can onto the table. "We had total privacy for our clubhouse until you and Nathan started messing around with a bike-a-thon."

"What clubhouse?"

"The hut by the old road off the side of the bike trail. No one was the least bit interested in that trail. It had grown up with weeds until you two got a brainwave."

"The trail has always been intended for bikes, whether it's been used or not."

"The point is, Matt, it wasn't being used. First, our leader decided that I could prove my loyalty to the gang if I took the bike of my cousin's best friend. He liked that bike."

"You? You took Nathan's bike?" Matt gulped for air. When Allie grinned, something snapped inside him and he yelled, "That doesn't make sense! Stealing one bike wouldn't stop a bike-a-thon."

"Nathan has a big ego. It might have worked. Especially when he didn't have the bike he showed off to the entire town."

"Nathan lost his legs because of that bike, Allie. Or have you missed that part?"

"Nathan lost his legs because he either raced a train or a truck hit him into the train. I had nothing to do with it."

Obviously, Allie thought it made perfect sense. "So what's the graffiti got to do with this?"

"Nothing. That was a fun night. What's really fun is that, as far as the police are concerned, they have you."

"You were seen. I wasn't."

"Fingerprints count in a courtroom more than an eyewitness."

"Who told you that?"

"Dean's experienced. I'll say I saw you and Nathan lurking around the alley and doing the graffiti."

Matt fought to just think straight after learning the Silver Bullet had been stolen by his own cousin. Now, her deliberate attack on him dug deep to the roots of family betrayal. His fingerprints plus Allie's testimony equalled a bad equation. Real bad.

Dean. Did he know a Dean? Throwing caution away, Matt flung her a surprise of his own. "Won't fly, Allie. I have you three on video."

Allie smiled sarcastically. "You don't expect me to fall for that one, do you? You'd have handed it in right away to protect your father. He's all stressed out."

In spite of panic burning in his chest, Matt steadied his eyes on her.

Allie laughed. "I guess the joke's on you. You're not a gang member, yet you're the only suspect. No wonder your dad is worried about you."

"I'd rather he worry about innocent me than a guilty niece who's special to him."

Allie stopped twirling the pop can and stared at Matt. He watched the skin pull tight around her eyes. "I guess gangs, illegal graffiti, and stealing bikes is more important to you than family right now. Especially when you knew I'd recognize those cans spread all over the trail. You really don't care about my dad? My dad who tutored you last summer so you didn't have to go to summer school and could still pass. My dad who taught you tennis."

Allie sat still. "Just let the bike-a-thon go, Matt, and everything will be all right."

He walked to the door, then turned around. "No it won't. You won't be all right. Your war with the bike-a-thon is wrong, Allie. You'll lose."

Matt walked home. Shock and betrayal cramped his thoughts into a headache. As he closed the door quietly behind him, he heard his parents talking in the kitchen about another graffiti. Thank goodness it happened last night. He'd been with his parents.

Dad sighed. "We just don't understand the fingerprints, yet. He's a good kid. I have to believe in him. He said he'd start delivering those papers for me yesterday."

"Do we know he has?"

Quenching an urge to run and hide the five hundred papers, Matt determined he'd start them tomorrow, for sure.

"Come on, Nina, since when has Matt ever dived into something promptly?"

Matt clanged the door handle. "I'm home!"

Turbo slid to the top of the stairs and bounded down to greet him.

That night, Matt looked at his clock every hour. Waves of worry crashed in his stomach every time the newest equation rolled through his thoughts. The theft, by his own cousin, plus the chase, equalled Nathan without legs. *His own cousin.*

Matt woke with a start at six in the morning. He rolled out of bed. As usual, he first checked his email. "Aha," he yawned with triumph. "Finally, Turbo, it's here."

The covers wiggled. Turbo popped out, one ear bent back, and he yawned, too.

> Dear Matt,
> Bicycling legs are not usually required for below the knee amputations. Pedal clips, to hold the toes in place, will probably be sufficient. Of course, the prosthetic foot must have easy release from the pedal to prevent injury in the case of falls.

"Yes!" Anyone who could make a can crusher could make pedal clips. That meant less money to raise and it took power out of Jeremy Miller's argument. He clicked the exit button and shut off the screen.

Downstairs in the kitchen, Mom rolled the top of his lunch bag. "Hi Mom. I'm leaving early to deliver Dad's papers on Mary Street."

"What a good idea. By the way, I have to go to the city tomorrow. I'll wait until after school if you want to visit Nathan."

"Thanks." He kissed her cheek. "Turbo's still asleep in bed."

"Go on. It won't hurt him to walk with me this morning."

Matt slipped on his backpack, picked up the papers, and headed across town. He stopped at the tracks. Concentrating on the sun, barely peeking at the heavily frosted town, he saw visions of Nathan's bloody leg and Allie standing beside it. He looked both ways, twice. The crisp air tingled in his nose, yet the smell from that night still burned in his memory. So, sending deep breaths out from his mouth, he watched columns of air race the gentle wind. By the time he reached the park, his head felt light. The trees stood naked with only a hint of green emerging on their branches. Beyond them stretched the hideous invasion of aluminum cans.

Matt pulled a tattered paper from his pocket. He squeezed the speech's third paragraph to memory while he delivered papers down the street, past the school, and back up the other side. By the time he walked through the school's front doors, he knew the first page.

Most people watched where they walked, but Martha Brown stumbled into him because she had her nose in a book. Only Martha could do this, then act surprised at a collision. "Oh! Sorry, Matt. How's the speech going?"

"I hate English, and memorizing is as easy as finding world peace."

"It'll be worth it. I convinced Theresa and Sally to ride. They each raised over twenty dollars this weekend. Both have stepfamilies who compete with each other."

"Wow."

"How much have you raised?"

"What?"

"For the bike-a-thon. You're riding, aren't you?"

"Of course. I've been so busy with speeches, and trail problems, and Nathan ... thanks for the reminder."

Martha searched a book and pulled out a card. "Don't be nervous about the speech. You're allowed one card. Write the first words of each paragraph on it and you'll sail through it."

The first bell rang. Matt took the card and slid his backpack off his shoulders. "Thanks. I better hurry. See you in class."

ON TUESDAY AFTER SCHOOL, Matt rode the elevator to Nathan's floor with the Turbo bag at his side. He turned at Nathan's door, his finger on the bag's zipper, when a wave of window cleaner hit his nostrils. Halting in his steps, his finger frozen on the zipper, he was met by a housekeeper inside the door. "Good morning," the man nodded. "I'm finished."

Matt closed the door behind him. To his surprise, Nathan's bed was empty.

"Hi," said Nathan from behind the curtain. He sat at a small desk with a computer on it. Today, he smiled.

"Where did you get this?"

"I made a deal with the recreation department. They brought me a computer to use in my room if I go down there twice a week once I have my new legs. Then no one will know I look funny."

"You don't look funny, Nathan. You look like a normal person without legs."

"Sure," he mumbled, clicking off the screen. "Where's my Turbo?"

Turbo's tail drummed the sides of the bag. Matt passed him to Nathan.

"How's our speech going?"

"I've memorized three paragraphs. At this rate, I should be ready next year."

"Any problems on the trail?" He rubbed Turbo's ears vigorously, but at Matt's silence, he glanced up. "I remember a note."

Matt sat down on the bed. A weight of defeat pressed his shoulders forward. "There are some problems."

"What's happened?" Below perfectly combed hair, Nathan's eyes were brighter. He looked like his old self.

Still, Matt hesitated. Nathan needed all his energy for walking, not worrying. After all, Nathan couldn't solve problems with the bike trail.

"I can handle it, Matt. Don't treat me like I'm fragile. My parents are doing fine in that department."

"Your parents spent day and night here while you almost died."

"I know and I love them. But that bike-a-thon is important to me and I'm not almost dead anymore." Nathan scrunched his nose, an old habit he had to make Matt laugh.

Matt laughed. Today, Nathan was the way he'd always been. It was almost like discussing a project in the school lunch room, only this time Matt talked and Nathan did most of the listening.

"So, you cut your chin on the bike trail?"

"Yeah. They dug a trench and filled it with leaves. The Township fixed it. Yesterday, Sarah and I picked up the cans. We took the bags to Tom's alley for safe-keeping. Your dad said he's going to recycle on Thursday."

The door banged. Matt scrambled for the duffle bag, and just as he stuffed Turbo into it, Frank poked his head around the curtain. Matt relaxed and sighed. "Frank, you scared me to death."

Frank winked. "I thought he was here when I saw the door shut. I parked my scooter across the doorway. We'll hear them move it before anyone comes in."

Matt handed Turbo back to Nathan, pulled a large white envelope from the bag and waited until Frank finished greeting Turbo. "What do you have there?" Frank asked.

"I wanted to ask you a favour since you know so many people here. I'm doing the bike-a-thon for Nathan and I haven't had much time to collect money from sponsors. I wondered if you'd ask around, and see if the staff would donate. Even a dollar would be great."

"A dollar! I'll hit them for two. I see how many Tim Hortons coffees they drink around here." Frank lifted a bony finger towards Nathan. "Why don't you take my scooter and ride the bike-a-thon too?"

Matt's excitement soared, until he looked at Nathan. The look said it all. Nathan wasn't going to ride where people, especially classmates, would see him without legs.

Frank shrugged. "Well, the offer's open to you. Let me know if you change your mind."

"Frank!" Felicia protested from the doorway. "You can't leave your scooter parked here."

"I know. In case there's an emergency."

Matt grappled with Turbo, who was engrossed with this new game of pop-up. Playfully, he growled, and Matt gulped down uncensored panic.

"That's correct, Frank. Something could be brewing."

Frank chuckled while Felicia made it through the door and announced, "Someone's here to see you, Nathan."

Nathan stuffed the glove into the bag. Matt, seeing Felicia glance at the bag, stopped pulling the zipper halfway and set the bag against the wall near the curtain. It was hard to look calm when your fingers were shaking.

From the other side of the curtain emerged a bicycle wheel. Matt gasped, soaking in every detail of the shiniest metallic blue bicycle he'd ever seen. "Wow!"

Tom, owner of the donut shop, proudly held the handlebars. "Nathan, this is for you."

Nathan squeaked, "For me?"

Frank, who seconds ago had returned to his bed and lay with ankles crossed, popped back out of bed.

Tom nodded. "For you. I'm so sorry about your accident with the Silver Bullet. You boys have worked hard on that trail and I knew you'd need a new bike. You may not be able to ride it yet, but if Matt here can stay ahead of those renegades around town, you'll probably have another bike-a-thon to ride in."

"It's a beauty. I can't believe you'd do this."

"Your first trip to the shop gets you and Matt hot chocolate on the house." Tom wheeled the bicycle close to Nathan. Matt touched the smooth cool color, as did Nathan.

Nathan smiled. "Thank you, Tom."

While Felicia snapped a photograph with a Polaroid camera, Matt smiled at Frank. Nathan's eyes sparked a hopeful light. At the camera's second flash, a loud knock interrupted the excitement. If it wasn't for the clacking of high-heeled shoes, none may have noticed.

Felicia's face mirrored blank surprise while Frank stared in the direction of the door, open-mouthed. Tom glanced backwards over his shoulder as a lady, sporting a fire-engine red blazer and black skirt, waltzed into the room.

Frank murmured under his breath, "Our Head Coordinator, boys."

In her arms, Turbo panted.

CHAPTER 7

IF PEOPLE COULD turn invisible, this would be the perfect time. However, Matt's body remained intact to the naked eye.

The Head Coordinator studied Turbo and rubbed his ears. She peered over narrow gold glasses and examined Nathan first, then Matt. "Do you recognize this adorable little fellow?" The fact she called Turbo adorable contradicted her piercing eyes.

Matt, struggling to breathe, never mind talk, listened as Frank cleared his throat. "I've seen him around. Cute as a button."

She pinned her eyes on Matt. "Does he belong to you?"

Matt's skin began to sweat and his voice faltered. "Not really."

Over the glasses, her eyes shifted to Nathan. "Is he yours?" she asked.

From the other side of the curtain, a male voice broke the silence. "Looks like a party." The man stopped beside the Head Coordinator, shifted two artificial legs to his left arm, and admired Turbo. He chuckled. "Pet therapy day, Mary?"

No one missed the sarcasm in her voice. "Apparently so, Daniel. Are these Nathan's new legs?"

"They are." His eyes glanced off of Matt's legs to the empty space below Nathan's knees. "Can I borrow Nathan for about ten minutes?"

Tom insisted he had donuts to bake. "Matt, we had this planned with your parents and Nathan's. Chuck's coming later with his truck to take you and the bike home."

Matt suspected the high-heeled Sergeant-Major had caught his name. With hopes dashed for a ride home with Tom, he surrendered himself to fate. At least Turbo had made Nathan smile again.

Tom shook Nathan's hand. "Nathan, I can't wait to see you back in town. All the best. Work hard." Tom left.

Felicia wheeled the bicycle to the wall and excused herself from the room. Frank sat down on Nathan's bed and watched.

The Coordinator wasn't very busy because she stroked Turbo while Daniel organized the legs and removed material from two bags. Meanwhile, con-artist Turbo had gone to sleep in enemy arms. That puppy was too friendly.

Kneeling down in front of Nathan, Daniel explained each step. "First, you slip this liner sock on the end of your legs this way. It protects your stumps from pain and sores."

He slipped the prosthetic leg over the sock. "Let's see how it looks with a shoe on." He did the same with the left leg and then pulled both pant legs down to the shoes.

Nathan nodded critically. "Not bad."

"Not bad?" Matt exclaimed. "You can't tell!"

"The shoes leave a lot to be desired."

Daniel's eyebrows shot up. "You like shoes? You can wear any shoe on your prosthetics."

"These are pretty bad. I want the pair I had."

A bloody mess shot through Matt's memory. He caught Daniel's eyes and shook his head vigorously.

"Ask your parents for a new pair. The old ones are probably too damaged from the accident."

"Probably burned with my legs."

The Coordinator pushed the curtain open to the wall. "Leave those legs on for me, Daniel. The three of us have a short trip to make. Your timing is impeccable." She smiled.

A nervous twitch sprinted across Matt's shoulders.

"Frank, would you please tell Felicia we need a wheelchair for Nathan?"

"Yes, Ma'am." On his way past her, Frank stroked Turbo. "Yep, cute as a button." Looking straight in her eyes, he winked. Frank shuffled forward.

Frank's voice carried from the nursing desk across the hall. "No sense rolling an empty wheelchair to the gallows, May. Let me hop in."

Gallows? That man oozed reassurance.

With a hand on each of Nathan's sides, Daniel instructed, "Stand up. I'll hold you steady. Feel your balance."

Matt imagined his own feet strapped to stilts, himself sitting on a tall stool and trying to stand. The first challenge would be to get vertical at all.

May slipped the wheelchair close beside Nathan. Daniel coached him. "Step sideways." Nathan's fingers dug into Daniel's arms while he inhaled and exhaled in the silence. "Good. Now, I'll let you down into the chair."

After a successful sit, Nathan sighed. "I made it."

Daniel smiled. "I'll talk to Dan in Physiotherapy and meet you back here in . . . say, twenty minutes?"

The Coordinator nodded. "Perfect. Matt, you push Nathan and follow me." Her heels clacked with her departure. She still carried Turbo.

Never having pushed a wheelchair before, Matt shifted his weight from one foot to the other, locking his elbows and straining until the chair turned out the door. They followed her into the elevator. "By the way, my name is Mrs. St. John." She pressed floor number two. "As Frank said, I'm the Coordinator of the fifth floor. This is my first day back from vacation."

Matt recalled his father's advice about first impressions. His stomach cramped.

"Are any of my staff in on this?"

They both answered immediately. "No."

"Just Frank."

Matt finally said yes. "But he's lonely. You can't blame him."

Mrs. St. John lowered her pointed chin and peered at him over her glasses. She obviously liked to do that. "Does Frank look like a lonely old man to you?"

Nathan coughed. In desperation, Matt quenched an urge to laugh and schooled his face into stone. It wasn't safe to answer that question.

They exited the elevator in the main lobby. Leaning to the right, Matt pushed the wheelchair across the ceramic tile. Vibrations shot through the handles into Matt's hands. It was exactly like the bicycles on the grid bridges in the park.

Mrs. St. John stopped ahead and waited for them. Matt groaned and said, "Great. Boneshaker Trail directly to Security."

Nathan muttered over his shoulder to him, "The worst they can do is call our parents and give us a warning. They can't throw us in jail for this. We're minors."

Matt sucked in a breath and pushed forward. Security waited on the other side of a desk.

"Matt and Nathan, I'd like you to meet Mark, Head of Security."

Of course. It couldn't be an ordinary security officer. It had to be the Head.

"This very important pet needs a Pet Pass. Matt and he will be frequent visitors while Nathan is here."

Mark stepped to the computer. His waist belt jangled with rings of keys, an intercom, and handcuffs. "We usually have visitors stop in the office to pick up the pass on each visit. Will this be a variation to that?"

"Yes, it will."

Matt peeked at Mrs. St. John. She smiled guardedly. "It'll be your responsibility, Matt, to clip that identification onto his collar each time you visit the hospital."

Matt agreed. Nathan nodded. Mark slipped the identification into a plastic pouch and clipped it to Turbo's collar. "Just like that."

Mrs. St. John held the door open until they passed through. She relinquished Turbo to Nathan at the elevators and bid them a good day. Nathan slumped further into the chair. "Let's get back to my room."

Frank, reclining on his bed, propped himself onto one elbow and peered at their feet. "I don't see any ball and chains. At least you weren't arrested."

They told Frank about the adventure as Daniel returned, accompanied by a young man. His arm muscles bulged against the sleeves of a white T-shirt.

"Nathan," said Daniel, "you've met Dan from Physiotherapy. He'll be working with you and your legs. I'll check next week to see how they're working for you unless I hear about a problem sooner."

As soon as Dan had his nose in his appointment book, Nathan furrowed his eyebrows. Matt recognized the challenge. Turbo ambled backwards from under the bed, directly into the back of Dan's leg. He growled, beat the glove back and forth, and growled louder.

As Dan spun around, he stepped on Turbo's paw. Hysterical yelps pierced the air and Dan stumbled backwards. He caught himself from falling, but his arm hit the call bell attached to the Nathan's bed and it ripped out of the wall. Immediately, it set off the emergency ring.

Turbo abandoned his glove. Four paws spun in vain on the waxed floor, but once turned around, he tore under the bed. Matt fumbled the cord while hurrying to plug it back into the wall. As Turbo refused to come out, Frank sank to his knees on the other side of the bed. The pup looked at Frank and tucked in his tail. Quivering, he lay down on his belly.

Felicia burst into the room. "Oh no, Frank! How did you fall?"

Frank tried to rise and couldn't. "I didn't fall. Give me a hand, will you?"

"Are you hurt?" Felicia asked. Dan fastened one hand above Frank's elbow and the other on his belt while Felicia protested. "Now I have to fill out a report that you were on the floor."

"I didn't fall, I'm telling you. I got down there on purpose. Make sure you put that on the report."

So, after Frank stood on his feet, Felicia tried to lure Turbo out. In the end, Matt crawled on his belly and scooped the puppy into his arms. Nathan laughed so hard, he rocked forward and back.

Matt's optimism sparked alive.

Dan picked up his book and wrote down Nathan's first physiotherapy appointment for the following week. Nathan's humour evaporated. He began twitching in his chair as if he sat on a bag of marbles. "Why can't I do it in here? I don't want to go downstairs with all those people."

"They're learning to use artificial limbs, like you."

Nathan shook his head stubbornly. "No, I'm not going down. You come here."

"You need the equipment in the gym. You're learning to walk all over again, Nathan. You'll need the parallel bars to steady yourself."

"They should have those bars set up in our rooms so we can practice all the time."

"The bars are thirty feet long."

"In the hall, then."

Matt pressed his lips together. Nathan had refused to sit in the lounge and the dining room. What difference would the hall be?

"Can Matt come with me?"

"He has school."

"He's off Friday. It's a PD Day."

Usually, Matt celebrated a day off school with flare. Pancakes soaked with real maple syrup for breakfast. Watching movies with Nathan. A soup and bagel at Tom's Donut Shop, compliments of Nathan's mom. Nathan couldn't know that this PD Day was possessed by a To-Do list. Thick silence descended in the room because Matt couldn't bring himself to disappoint Nathan.

Dan stood up. "You discuss that possibility and I'll return in ten minutes."

Nathan stared at Matt. "You can't come Friday?"

"Nathan, I . . . I want to, but . . ."

"But what? We always spend PD Days together."

"I know . . . but I need to deliver my dad's ads for the campaign, and copy off the bike-a-thon ads and deliver them. I haven't memorized all the speech yet."

Nathan pressed his lips together in a tight line.

Guilt.

Personal success is doing your best because it's deep in your heart to do it.

But, Matt questioned, could spending time with a best friend be personal success if it was in his heart to do it—even if it took away from other promises?

His To-Do list flashed three words. Delivery, delivery, memorize. Two of those three words blazed a new idea. "What if I bring in *both* ads on Monday after school? We could sort them into pairs, then I could deliver them together in one trip instead of two. It's a lot of papers, but—"

"Okay!" Nathan quickly agreed.

That night, Matt stared out his bedroom window at a bright half moon. With his heart connected to God, he sensed God's hand reaching down from heaven and inching personal success a step closer. He whispered, "This is the hardest thing I've ever done."

By Sunday evening, Matt had memorized most of the speech. His stomach ached. The bike-a-thon depended on this speech, tomorrow.

He slipped his hands behind his head on his pillow. The down-filled comforter hugged him, but he tossed and turned anyway.

Mom slept in Monday morning, and because Matt couldn't fall asleep until three in the morning, he slept in too. At Mom's first cry to wake up, Matt bolted out of bed. Grabbing the clock, he thought for one horrible second that he'd slept past the rally. It turned out he'd missed math, but he had lots of time to get to school for the speech. He gulped down a hot chocolate and tried to clear his head. Sleeping past the rally might have relieved anxiety at one time, but he had a deal to keep. And Jeremy Miller would torment him forever if he slept through it.

When he arrived at school, Mrs. Bailey stopped writing on the blackboard, set the chalk down and came to stand in front of him. "Think of your heart issue."

"I'm not sure I remember what it is."

"Sure you do. Think hard."

"I'm not like my dad. I'm not a politician who likes to give speeches."

"But you're a best friend who's doing it for your best friend. You're doing it for children who have no playground equipment. You may not have your father's natural ability to speak, but some of these students may need to hear why the bike-a-thon is important. It could be that simple."

Nothing was simple.

Together, they walked to the auditorium where the voices of one hundred and fifty students increased as they approached the open double doors of the gymnasium. With each step, Matt's heart pounded faster. He drew in a deep breath, desperate for calm and unable to grasp it.

From the platform, Matt stared at the sea of faces while Mrs. Bailey introduced him. Stepping to the microphone, he opened his mouth. Nothing came out. Urgently, he cleared his throat and managed the official greeting.

The smooth enhancement of his voice resounded clearly in his own ears as he described little Thomas' play horse, a.k.a. a rusted wagon from the dump. Natasha's older brother had nailed a slide onto a log since its broken stand was left behind at the dump. "The nails let go, but he won a prize—an arm cast."

Sarah, wearing her purple school shirt, laughed. Martha Brown did a thumbs-up with all rings glittering. Momentarily, Matt's mind blanked, until Mrs. Bailey smiled encouragement.

Matt glanced at his card. The word 'James' refreshed his momentum.

"James, three-years old, smiles like a world traveler in a bright yellow plastic car—without wheels. It came from the dump too."

Matt paused for the last part of the speech. As soon as he spoke Nathan's name, the laughter faded. The room stilled and silence grew, except for the air rushing through the ventilation system. When he reported Nathan had walked on artificial legs between parallel bars last Friday, they clapped.

"Our total goal for swings, slides, and bicycle clips is eleven hundred dollars and fifty cents. If we add one dollar to another dollar, we can make our goal. Come out on June first. Be a boneshaker, and ride Boneshaker Trail for the kids. Or bring your bike and ride for moral support. I hope to see you there."

They applauded and Matt stepped back. The principal, Mr. Tyndale, praised him for a speech well done and supporting worthy causes. He reminded grades four and five they were to return to the gymnasium after lunch for a guest speaker. "You're dismissed for lunch."

Matt slipped to his locker because he'd forgotten the money Mom gave him for his lunch since they'd slept in. Sarah ran up to him in the french fries line up. "I think my whole gym class is going to do the ride. Mrs. Brown said whoever goes can count it as part of their mark."

Martha Brown jostled in behind Sarah. "You won't believe this, but Jeremy might ride. I heard him with my own ears."

Winston Woodingham tapped Matt on the shoulder. "My father wants to know about receipts for tax purposes. And is there going to be a nurse on duty like at camp?"

Martha scoffed at him. "Tell your dad this isn't a government organization. It's just a fund-raiser for some kids." She sniffed. "Honestly."

Matt took his fries, gulped down a few, and joined classmates at a table near the doors. Had the attitude really shifted in support of the bike-a-thon, or was it just hopeful thinking on his part?

After lunch, Matt's group headed to the gymnasium. When he glanced at the stage and saw two police officers setting up a presentation, he stopped dead in his tracks. "What's the topic?"

"Gangs." Martha sailed away to sit in the front row, as usual.

Matt flopped into a second row seat before he fell down. The Officers probably knew exactly who he was even though it wasn't Officers Ray or Mary. As students filed in, Jeremy sat in the front row and nodded to Matt over his shoulder. "Good speech, Timmotay."

"Thanks."

Well, Matt decided, he'd block his ears and concentrate on the ride. They had four booths to set up along the trail. He had to print the tickets from Nathan's computer that the riders would have punched at each booth to mark off their distance completed.

Mr. Tyndale introduced the two officers.

Cartoons splashed onto the screen from the overhead projector and dived into topics such as respect and responsibility. Integrity jumped out at Matt—being faithful to good principles—because Allie was certainly challenging that subject. On the other hand, was he being faithful to good principles when he knew who had done the graffiti to Tom and who had influenced the accident? In fact, hadn't he done graffiti to the bicycle seat?

Officer Teresa walked off the stage and across the front row of seats. Matt slid down further into his chair. She put a microphone to her mouth. "Who knows the difference between telling and squealing?"

Matt looked around him without moving his head. Martha should know.

"Anyone want to take a guess?"

Jeremy's hand went up. "They're the same."

"They both mean you're reporting something, don't they? The difference is the intention behind it. Telling is simply reporting facts. Squealing is reporting facts because you want the other person to get into trouble."

The last thing Allie needed was more trouble than she already had. Whether Matt told without intention or squealed with intention, Allie would still have more trouble.

The Officers used the bike-a-thon as an example of the school's cooperation to reach a common goal and respecting the worth and dignity of others by showing kindness and compassion. "We have to do our part in projects like this, in school, and in society. Gangs work against all of that. They may make someone feel important, but many gang members go on to break the law, assault, and serve jail terms. Bad things often happen as a result of their activity, even if they don't intend it."

That summed up the past month in a nut shell. Allie didn't feel important. She didn't think her parents even knew her favourite meal. She may not have intended the train accident, Ball Cap probably didn't, but it had happened because they stole a bicycle.

Matt asked permission to leave school early that day. At home, he crawled into bed and slept until Mom called him for supper.

Chapter 8

Saturday morning marked two weeks to the bike-a-thon. At the trail entrance, Matt set his bicycle's odometer to zero and measured the distance to the first check-in point. While he pushed an orange flag into the ground, Turbo sniffed the thickening ground cover. With his ears perked up straight, he hedged behind a wild grape vine as a large oak leaf skittered near him. He jumped out of hiding onto the leaf as the head of Ball Cap surfaced from the steep ravine on the other side of the path.

Matt blinked, hoping to clear his vision. Ball Cap looked up. Spotting Matt, he huffed towards him while beads of sweat rolled down his ghostly white face. "You're done now, Timmotay."

Because Turbo showed poor judgment in who he befriended, Matt picked him up. Keeping a safe distance from Ball Cap, he scoffed, "Maybe you should catch your breath before dishing out threats."

Ball Cap fumbled a red candy wrapper and popped the toffee into his mouth. "Told the police you're my main man."

Even if Matt believed Ball Cap, and actually, he did, Matt determined he would not give satisfaction to either him or Allie. Although the inside of a jail looked more real than ever, Matt rolled his eyes and put on his best bored face.

Ball Cap frowned. "Dean tore it down."

"Dean tore what down?"

"Not Dean. I know it was you." Ball Cap wiggled a shaky finger at Matt and yelled, "You, Matt Timmotay!"

Turbo startled and growled. Matt hugged him close as he wiggled, and judged the distance to his bicycle.

Ball Cap turned away. He stumbled over a vine, and disappeared down the path.

Matt stared after him. Did Ball Cap ever act sensible? With an eye over his shoulder, Matt rode in the opposite direction and marked the other two check-in points.

On Monday morning after English class, Mrs. Bailey asked Matt to return after school to discuss his speech mark. Her manner, as innocent as Turbo sleeping, shifted at the end of the day. She leaned against her desk with Matt's speech in her left hand, but her right hand made his composure tremble. It rested on her hip.

"You worked very hard memorizing this speech."

"Yes, Mrs. Bailey."

"I clearly remember explaining how I'd calculate the mark: forty percent written, forty percent memorization, and twenty percent for presentation. You couldn't have known that Nathan discussed his speech with me."

A heat wave flooded Matt's body while one thought raced around in his mind. Had Nathan remembered this one tiny detail, Matt would have tackled the project in a whole different way. He swallowed the lump in his throat. "I only wrote the last part."

"You memorized it well. Your presentation was excellent. The part you wrote proves you're better at English than you give yourself credit for. However, I could only give you a C."

Considering he had planned to skip the speech altogether, which would have earned him a zero, that sounded fine. In fact, he was proud of a C.

"But I've decided the mark is incomplete until you write an essay on the finished bike-a-thon."

Matt's heart somersaulted, startling him out of his proud C. "An essay?"

"It's hard to top the importance of this bike-a-thon or the reasons you're doing it. As a student, you have to do as fine a job with integrity. I want to see your work, not Nathan's. Your essay will count as your forty percent. I'll expect it one week after the Ride." She nodded dismissal.

"Yes, Mrs. Bailey."

Matt hardly saw the custodians mopping the silent halls or the deserted school yard. At home, he slipped into blue jeans and played in the yard with Turbo until Dad finished his phone call. This bike-a-thon had complicated his life.

"Ready, Matt?" Dad asked, car keys in his hand and a brown envelope in his mouth. "I'm in a hurry."

"We're ready."

At the front doors of the hospital, Matt clipped on Turbo's Pet Pass. With his enthusiasm bruised, he dropped off the two boxes of advertisements in the auditorium and dragged his feet to the fifth floor. Mrs. St. John passed him at the Nurse's station. She patted Turbo's head and smiled approval at his identification.

Matt steeled himself to be optimistic. Sucking in a deep breath at Nathan's door, he pushed away the day's negatives. After all, what was an essay after memorizing that speech?

Nathan lay on his bed, sleeping. Last Friday, Felicia had said she'd help him put on his legs before she left on Monday at three o'clock. Nathan's legs sat against the wall.

All the negatives crashed in on Matt. His shoulders sagged.

Turbo scampered up the bed and licked Nathan's chin. "Hi Matt." Nathan laughed between licks. "Felicia left a photo album on the desk for you."

Not ready to argue with Nathan about the legs, Matt opened the album. A child's clear brown eyes stared up at him from an eight by ten photograph. On the next page, an older couple and a baby smiled at each other. Page after page, Felicia's photography captured candid close-ups. The similar style to Matt's photography flooded him with regret. He'd planned to do exactly this for the bike-a-thon. They had started to do it, but then the accident happened.

Was there time to do a photo shoot at the apartment building this weekend? He could set up a photo display at school during the final week for the die-hard sceptics. Jeremy had raised almost thirty-five dollars. If Jeremy planned to ride, there was hope for anyone.

Matt glanced at Nathan as he closed the album. "Ready to go?"

Silence. A knot tightened in Matt's stomach.

"I can't go today. I'm too tired."

"Is it the phantom pain?"

"No, not really. I'm still weak."

"You promised me you'd help. I have to get the papers out."

"Let's do it here."

"Nathan, the auditorium's long tables are perfect to organize the papers on for the sections of town."

"I can't walk like you, going up and down between tables."

Frank clicked on his television, crossing his ankles. "Take my scooter."

"That won't help."

Matt looked Nathan square in the eye. "You're breaking a promise."

"I never promised to go to the auditorium."

"You agreed Felicia would put your legs on today before she went home so we could go to the auditorium. You won't go anywhere."

"You're not so perfect, playing Mr. Fix-it for everyone. Busy, busy, busy, fixing everything."

"Am not."

"Are too."

"Am not."

"You're so busy fixing your dad, you need help to deliver his papers."

"Because I came here last Friday on my PD day," argued Matt.

"Playing Mr. Fix-it."

"No. I came as a friend. You lost your legs, Nathan, not your brain. Just be you."

"You be you. You're doing the bike-a-thon, but you don't have the same reasons as I did."

"Because the Ride is your project, not mine."

"So what's yours? You were second-in-command."

"Taking photos to advertise. You know that."

"And where are they?"

Because of the silence on their side of the room, the television's advertisement blared. Nathan folded his arms across his chest and stared at Matt without blinking.

Matt wasn't sure if this was about steroids or losing legs, but one thing he knew, it wasn't about pictures. His anger with Nathan evaporated. "I realized that as I looked at Felicia's photo album."

Nathan's arms relaxed and he mumbled, "Me too."

Matt plopped down on the chair at the computer desk. "I just can't do it all. So, what's your plan? Are you going to help me accomplish the bike-a-thon or make me feel guilty because I'm Mr. Fix-it?"

"I'm different."

A cart rattled down the hall. Not wanting to provoke Nathan further, Matt chose his words carefully. "Dr. Farley said you'll do things differently. Not having legs is a forever change, but your brain is still Nathan Nadeau."

"Well . . . Felicia's gone home. The nurses are busy giving out pills. Maybe later this week."

"I don't have the rest of the week. We can put the legs on. It's not as if you're going to walk. You do one and I'll do the other."

Frank groaned from his side of the room.

Nathan bristled. "I'll do it myself."

"I can help," insisted Matt.

"I'll do it myself. I'll show both of you."

"Nathan . . .."

"I said I can do it myself! They're my legs. I'm not stupid."

"Fine," snapped Matt. Throwing up his hands, he stomped out of the room. In the hall, he leaned against the wall. With his feelings hurt, he argued with himself what to do next. He wanted to tell Nathan to forget it, that he'd sort the papers himself. It would serve Nathan right if he felt guilty about that.

Just as he decided to tell Nathan he didn't have to come down to the auditorium, Mrs. St. John exited her office near the nurse's station. She had a jacket and purse over one arm.

"Everything okay, Matt?"

Matt almost snapped it was a perfect day if one liked torture, but instead, he sighed. Half of the day's misery he'd brought upon himself. "Nathan's putting on his legs."

"Does he need help?"

"He has to do this on his own."

Annoyed groans and complaints spilled into the hall. Nathan snarled, "Can't they make something simple enough to slip on?" A thump echoed. Then a bang. "I hate them!"

Mrs. St. John looked over her glasses at the door. "It sounds like he needs help."

Matt sighed and straightened up. He tip-toed one step at a time into the room and peered around the curtain.

Nathan spotted him right away. He glowered. "Can't you give me a lousy five minutes? I told you, I'm not stupid."

Matt stepped back into the hall, clenching his teeth. He exchanged looks with Mrs. St. John. She nodded. "Perhaps you're right. Nathan needs to do this by himself. Good night, Matt."

"Good night, Mrs. St. John."

After fifteen minutes of grunts and groans, the scooter beeped in reverse. Matt knew Frank had had enough.

Frank's scooter shot through the doorway like a bowling ball. Nathan's legs sprawled in the air and his spine leaned severely over the seat. Nathan stopped six inches from the opposite wall in the hall. His bulging eyes mirrored horror.

Frank hollered, "Better put that dial on turtle speed before you land on the moon."

While Nathan studied the dials, Matt dashed into the room for Turbo, his leash, and the glove. He exchanged a nervous wink with Frank. Spotting Nathan's eyeglasses, he grabbed them too, and met Nathan in the hall as he successfully turned the scooter away from the wall. Set on turtle speed, the scooter rolled serenely to the elevators.

After Matt opened one of the auditorium's double doors, he pressed himself against the wall for Nathan to drive past. Nathan hesitated. "Open the other door too."

Matt set Turbo on Frank's hand towels in the scooter's basket. The other door of the auditorium had a lock at the top. Try as he might, he couldn't reach the catch. "Can't you go through on super turtle?"

"If I back up, you could stand on the bumper."

Remembering the wild departure from Nathan's room, Matt ignored that suggestion and used a chair to reach it. Nathan rode around the empty room while Matt pulled two tables together. He had just set out the two boxes of papers to be sorted when Nathan complained of thirst. "Could you go back to my room and get my ice water?" They stared at each other for a second. Nathan added, "Please."

Mom sometimes said she counted to three so she wouldn't explode. Matt counted to three—silently. "Be right back." The center elevator door opened and he waited while a hospital worker rolled the laundry bin passed him. Matt slipped in and pressed the fifth floor button. He tapped one foot.

To Matt's surprise, a set of rear doors opened on the fifth floor. Peeking out, scooters by the dozen lined the corridor. Walking past eight of them, he gained his bearings in the main hall and found Nathan's room three doors to the left.

After Frank's initial surprise, he waved a ten dollar bill to Matt. "If you can prod Nathan to the cafeteria, and that might be a trick, bring me back a medium black coffee and buy yourselves a hot chocolate."

Matt retraced his steps to the door of the back hall. With no one in sight, he slipped through the door. Nearest the elevator sat a turquoise scooter. Like the others, it had a key in it, but this one sat unplugged. It didn't have a basket, so he set the water jug between his feet, turned the key on, set the dial to turtle, and drove onto the rear elevator.

When Matt arrived in the auditorium, Nathan's mouth dropped open. A grin spread across his face. "Let's get these papers done and go outside for a ride."

Matt decided it risky to hold his breath on that suggestion. As far as he could tell, coming off steroids was one wicked ordeal.

They finished the papers in half an hour. With Turbo and his glove in the basket, they rode the elevator to the main floor, past Security, and out the front doors of the hospital.

With the wind in their hair and the sun in the west warming their faces, they headed down the hospital road. Matt, wondering if Security would be on the chase at any moment, swerved around the massive water puddle in the middle of the road. Nathan veered opposite, bumping across potholes, but avoiding the puddle. Back on course, they sped down the hill to the traffic lights.

Turbo dropped his glove outside the basket and Matt had to retrieve it. Without any sign of Security, they flicked the dials to rabbit and sailed to the nearby Mall.

Matt bought the drinks while Nathan waited outside with Turbo. Between sips of hot chocolate, Nathan rallied around a photograph poster. "You could display it at school all week then set it up at the park. It'll make it real to the riders." Before returning to the hospital, Matt bought a poster board. With it rolled in a bag between his feet, they rode back to the hospital in the cool of the day. The sun, big and red, touched the horizon.

A van with a CJP Newspaper decal on the side of it drew alongside them. "Hey, boys," greeted a black-haired man with black rimmed glasses. He held up his camera. "My name is Drew Moore. You're a perfect picture to celebrate a bright spring day like today."

Who could say no to that? They sat on their scooters under a nearby cherry tree heavy with unopened blossoms. Turbo refused to drop the glove, but otherwise he sat in the basket with perfect poise for the camera.

Drew snapped three photos. "So, what's got you outside today?"

"Shopping," said Matt. "We're doing a bike-a-thon in our town in two weeks and we needed a poster board."

"Raising money for school?"

Nathan explained about the children who needed play equipment. The more he talked, the brighter he grew. By the time the newsman left, the air blew cold and Nathan rubbed the end of his left leg. "The phantom pain is worse in the cold and my pills are due. We better hurry before they page us."

In agreement, Matt accelerated up the hill at rabbit velocity and topped the incline first. The massive water puddle, still in the middle of the road where they'd last seen it, rushed at him. Matt squeezed every muscle of his body tight as a spring and jammed the handles to the right. The scooter swung hard, throwing his right leg up into the air. A wave of water splashed over the scooter's base and ice cold water soaked his left foot and leg. Matt bellowed over his shoulder, "PUDDLE!"

Too late.

Nathan shot straight into the puddle's center. All four wheels lurched down into its depths, shooting out waves in all directions. His hair dripped water down his face, behind the eyeglasses, and from the lenses. Looking at his shoes, he scowled and his mouth drew into a tight line.

Matt rushed over and seized a towel from under the wet ones in the basket. He rubbed down Turbo, then did the same to Nathan's hair and glasses and the ugly shoes. Nathan protested, "Ugly, yes. But at least they cover the phony feet from the world's eyes."

Since a prosthetic foot looked like a thick wooden shoe, Matt had to agree. He kicked off his own shoes, and one at a time, poured water from them. He turned his back to Nathan. Forcing his feet back into wet shoes sent shudders of discomfort up his spine. Back in the room on the fifth floor, Matt slipped Frank's coffee from the wet bag. "At least your coffee was safe."

Frank fussed over Turbo. "You look like you went through a car wash."

Matt wiped the poster board in the bathroom, thankful it splashed on the rough side. Frank asked Nathan how he'd rate his day on a scale of one to ten.

Matt calculated the obvious. Subzero. Probably minus five.

"It was the best!" exclaimed Nathan.

The hospital paging system announced, "Matt Timmotay, please meet your party at the front foyer. Matt Timmotay."

Frank waved a hand at Nathan. "Matt has to go. You better head down the hall to the linen cart and get a couple towels. You don't want your legs to rust."

Matt squelched his way to the main hospital doors. He slid onto the front seat of Dad's car and wiggled his shoulders, trying to loosen tight muscles. In spite of a day of torture, Nathan had mobilized. Matt squeezed his eyes shut and prayed it would last.

Dad folded his paper and stopped whistling. "How was your visit?"

"It was Nathan's best day."

"Hmm." He turned the key in the ignition. "And you?"

"My worst."

Chapter 9

ON WEDNESDAY, Chuck stopped by Matt's house on his way home from work. He held up a new bicycle helmet. "These vibrant blue swirls match the new bicycle. Nathan wants to see you. He has a surprise. Can you go?"

Matt thought of a dozen reasons to stay home, the best one being until Nathan was discharged home. He just couldn't say the words. "I'll get Turbo."

At the hospital, Nathan glowed. He pointed to five newspapers on his bed. "We're front page and center."

Matt studied the photograph and laughed at Turbo in the basket. The glove hung nearly as big as the puppy.

"This is great advertising," Nathan reasoned. "I might ride Frank's scooter in the bike-a-thon. Matt, will you ride the new bike? I'm calling it Blue Lightning."

Ride Blue Lightning! Nathan's excitement might flip opposite before the bike-a-thon, but Matt shrugged away his doubt. "I'd love to ride it."

The wall speaker clicked once, then a second time. "Matt and Nathan, this is Mrs. St. John. I'd like to see you both in my office at four ten."

Matt whispered to Chuck. "What time is it?"

The speaker answered. "Four-o-eight."

"Yes, Mrs. St. John."

"Nathan?"

"It might take me four minutes to get into the wheelchair."

"Your father will assist you. Legs aren't necessary. See you in one minute, thirty seconds."

"Yes, Mrs. St. John."

Matt waited until the light on the speaker box blinked out. He whispered urgently, "Have we done something?"

Frank pulled the curtain back, sporting a smile.

It crossed Matt's mind to slip down the back elevator, but Mrs. St. John had obviously seen them arrive and she'd as easily recognize an escape in progress. One minute and thirty seconds later, she towered over them in her small office. Matt sat down in a nearby chair. She closed the door behind Nathan's wheelchair. "Nice newspaper article."

"Thank you," said Nathan.

"I know where your scooter came from, Nathan, and I'm sure Frank gave you permission to use it."

"He did."

When Mrs. St. John smiled, fine lines beside her eyes crinkled. "If we'd known a scooter would move you out of your room, we'd have offered you one long ago."

Matt grimaced. It'd taken more than a scooter to root him out of that room, as Frank would attest to, but there wasn't time to dwell on that because Mrs. St. John stared at him. She didn't even blink. Matt held up a hand. "I know. I didn't ask permission. I'm sorry."

"Good. That's cleared up. Now, hospital Security is concerned about liability. That's when the hospital is responsible if there's an accident. One way around that is to pass the hospital's scooter training program. Someone from Occupational Therapy would review a scooter with each of you and assess you on a trip outdoors. Interested?"

"Sure," said Matt at the same time as Nathan.

"Good. I'll arrange it. It's been a pleasure, gentlemen. Thank you."

Later, at the supper table, Matt showed his parents the newspaper he brought home with him. "It's a good article on the bike-a-thon."

"And a terrific picture," Mom gushed. "And look at that Turbo." Ten minutes later, when Officers Mary and Ray sat in their living room, Mom's glow vanished.

Officer Ray, opening his own copy of the newspaper, held it up to Matt. He said, "Tell us about this glove."

The glove? The glove! A chill inched straight to Matt's bones.

Mom's face paled to the shade of Aunt Kay's white roses on the table beside her. Dad slid an ankle over one knee and leaned back in the chair, staring at Matt. Matt's tongue stuck to his mouth like Velcro.

"Last Monday, we talked with Cameron Smith, otherwise known as Ball Cap."

Matt forced his tongue over his teeth. "You believe guys with a record? It's my word against theirs?"

Officer Ray snapped, "You have fingerprints on a paint can. You possess a glove exactly like one retrieved at the crime scene. That's called evidence, Matthew."

Dad leaned forward and pleaded, "Matt, let's deal with this. Anyone can get hooked up with a couple of bad characters, but let's straighten this out. I'd rather we get you help now than when it's too late."

Unfortunately, "too late" had come. A glance at the newspaper flashed a far different headline across Matt's imagination. "Local Politician suffers relapse of depression when only son and favoured niece are jailed as Young Offenders." Matt knew if he told on Allie, she'd claim he'd been there. They had fingerprints. And they now connected a glove to him. The evidence outweighed his video clip.

Matt cleared his throat. "Does this mean jail?"

Officer Mary answered. "Cameron qualifies for a program that educates Young Offenders. His buddy doesn't. There's a girl involved, but Tom only saw her pink hair, not her face."

Dad's voice cracked. "Pink hair?"

Officer Mary shrugged. "It doesn't mean much. Go down to the Junior High school and you'll see half a dozen pink hairdos standing around."

Matt shifted his feet. A "program" sounded similar to school. "Would I qualify?" he asked.

Immediately, Mom groaned. Matt steadied his eyes on Officer Mary.

Officer Ray stood up. He blocked Matt's view of his parents, but his voice filled every corner of the room. "Matt's age and the lack of being directly witnessed will no doubt eliminate him as a first time offender."

Just as a huge wave of relief washed over Matt, Dad rubbed a hand over his face. "Yes, and that doesn't help him at all, does it?"

"Not a bit."

Matt's chest tightened like it had been passed through Uncle Ted's can crusher. He wanted to scream about his innocence. He wanted to scream, "Not fair!" With only some of the facts, Dad believed him guilty. Nathan lost his legs over his own bicycle. And, it might be a rotten thing that Uncle Ted and Aunt Kay didn't know spaghetti was Allie's favourite meal, but lying about your cousin wasn't fair, either.

Mom walked the Officers to the door and never returned. Dad's blank eyes rushed in a wave of guilt. He opened his mouth to tell all, then closed it. He'd feel as guilty telling Dad the hurtful news about Allie.

God's business of doing miracles had kept Nathan alive and his dad depression-free, so in spite of the unfairness, Matt determined to keep his part of the bargain. "I'll do what I can to clear this up."

"Matt..."

"You've done good for two years without depression."

"Matt, some depressions are caused from events that happen in life, but I have an imbalance in my body with certain chemicals. The pills keep me balanced."

"But after Uncle John died . . . ?"

"I was already headed into a depression when he died. Is that what this is about? You've tried to protect me from depression?"

"Problems are stressful."

"If stress caused my depression, I'd have to give up politics." Dad leaned forward, elbows on his knees. "Why are your fingerprints on a paint can? How did you get that glove?"

Matt's eyes shot around the room until they rested on the family photo wall. Like Nathan, his family had changed a lot. Uncle John, dead. Cousin Edward, Allie's brother, lived in an institution. Allie's happy smile, erased.

"Are you protecting Allie?"

Matt forced a tight smile. "All I can say is I wouldn't hurt Tom. I hope you believe that."

ON SATURDAY MORNING, after Matt snapped a dozen photos at the low-income building, he rode straight to the photo center where he handed over his camera card. Then, he picked up Blue Lightning from the Nadeaus. With Turbo under his arm, he sped to Tom's Donut Shop. Tom stood outside talking to Grandpa Nadeau.

Matt announced to the men, "Nathan's going to ride in the bike-a-thon."

Grandpa Nadeau's eyes widened. "You don't say."

"He's riding Frank's purple scooter." Matt patted Blue Lightning's handlebar. "I'm riding Blue Lightning."

Tom nodded with pride. "Thatta boy."

Minutes later, Matt's feet spun the pedals of Blue Lightning. It whispered around the bike trail. He scouted around for Ball Cap, but the trail looked in order. Perhaps they'd given up.

Late in the day, Matt left Turbo at home and sped on his own bicycle to pick up the photographs and his card. Blue Lightning sat secure in the garage, "lock, stock, and barrel," as Grandpa Nadeau would say.

Outside the drug store, Matt flipped through the photos. Michael, in perfect focus, smiled at his scratched and dented ball. Lorissa sat on her slide with big blue eyes sparkling between blonde pigtails. Her brother's cast arm lay over her shoulder. Matt's chest swelled with euphoria. He loved photography.

Two-year-old toddlers, standing side by side, exchanged secret looks. Sarah, her hair over her shoulder, leaned into the wind over her handlebars. The aerial shot didn't capture the emotion he'd intended. When he flipped it to the back of the pile and saw the next photograph, his bottom jaw dropped.

He and Nathan sat on the lower branch of the octopus tree—laughing. Because Sarah had snapped the photo from the ground, their legs showed enormous detail.

Nathan's legs. Legs he tried hard to remember. Legs they'd never see again.

As soon as he arrived home, he tucked the important photograph into his top drawer.

In spite of the five-day forecast predicting rain for the bike-a-thon, Matt and Nathan sped on scooters to the hospital auditorium. They'd passed their scooter course. Today, they painted posters and banners for the trail stations.

Nathan washed his paintbrush in the jar of water. "When is your Dad putting these up?"

"Friday afternoon. When do you come home on Friday?"

"Dad's picking me up at three. Mrs. St. John told Frank he can use your scooter that weekend since he's letting me use his. I come back to the hospital Sunday evening."

"Are you nervous?"

"I'd rather give a speech. Will you be at the house on Friday when I come home? In case I have trouble walking with the crutches?"

Matt hesitated. "Is that being Mr. Fix-it?"

Worry lines creased Nathan's forehead. "As my friend."

Matt smiled. Soon, things would be almost normal again. "I'll be there. And on Saturday, I'll take a picture of you at the park on Frank's scooter and give it to him. I couldn't have raised fifty dollars by myself."

So, on Friday afternoon, Matt stood in the Nadeau's front yard with Sarah, Grandma and Grandpa. They weren't alone. Many of the neighbours had gathered in their front yards.

The cloudy sky promised rain. Matt spoke low to Sarah. "This whole project has been one problem after another. Of course it'll rain."

Chuck's truck turned the corner and all sorts of noise erupted. Grandma Nadeau sobbed into a tissue while neighbours waved and whistled and shouted greetings. Sarah smiled. "This is good, even though it'll never be like it was."

"Just different," said Matt, his throat thicker than normal.

Nathan waved a hand out the window, a grin so big that Matt could see it before the truck parked in the driveway. Matt didn't trust his voice. He felt like crying a bit himself, so he smiled his biggest silent smile.

Nathan flung open his door and stuck a leg into the air. "Look at these shoes!"

Everyone laughed, including Nathan.

After supper, Matt told his parents, "Nathan and I are going through the trail so he can see it. Is it okay if I go now?"

Dad scrambled to remove his cell phone from his pocket. "If there's any problem with Nathan's scooter, give me a call."

"Thanks." He slipped the phone inside the pouch of the camcorder. After a last-minute check that the camera held the bike-a-thon disc, he slipped the strap over his neck. Matt ran into the garage and stopped dead in his tracks. His eyes peeled around the room—twice. Heavy dread in his chest shook the illusion into reality.

Blue Lightning was gone.

When he raced into the kitchen, Mom spun around from the sink. "What on earth—"

"Nathan's bike has been stolen! It's gone."

"Don't be silly, dear. You told Allie she could borrow it this afternoon. She probably still has it."

"Allie? Allie Timmotay?"

"Yes, your cousin, Allie. What's the matter?"

Matt raced to the living room. "Where's Dad?"

Mom hesitated in the hall. "He's gone to the Post Office."

Matt ran out the front door as Dad turned left at the stop sign. At the end of the sidewalk, he clenched his fists at his side. A moment later, he relaxed them. "Allie, you're in over your head." He sighed. "Well, it's your head . . ."

Matt fetched his bicycle from the garage and sped to Allie's house. Three bicycles stood in the front yard near Aunt Kay's rose garden, but Blue Lightning was not one of them. Matt slipped inside the front door.

Silence.

The roses' perfume drifted through the open window and the curtain billowed in the light breeze. He heard angry murmurs in the backyard as he slipped through the kitchen and into the garage.

At the bottom of the step, Blue Lightning stood so close to him, he actually put a triumphant hand on it.

Quietly, he lifted the kickstand. Since the automatic garage door would make noise, Matt guided Blue Lightning to the kitchen.

He paused and peeked out the back door. Ball Cap and Dean lounged in the grass under the cherry tree. Allie reasoned, "We have the bike. That's enough revenge."

Dean scowled. "Not by a long shot. It's because of them we don't have our clubhouse anymore. They have to pay, big time."

Ball Cap popped a candy into his mouth. "Yeh, big time."

Dean pointed a finger at Allie. "This is your fault. If your cousin and his friend weren't such goody-two-shoes, we'd still have our hut."

Allie stood silent.

Matt wheeled the bicycle through the house and out the front door. Walking between two bicycles, he traveled to the Nadeau's house as fast as he could.

Nathan sat on the scooter in the driveway. "What are you doing?"

"There's trouble. Allie told my mom this afternoon she could borrow Blue Lightning, which I never said, and I've just taken it out of her garage. She's at her house with

Ball Cap and Dean. I think they're going to trash the check-in stations. We'd better get over there."

"Allie wouldn't do that."

"She does what Dean tells her to do. I'm leaving your bike here so it's safe. We'll be right back."

They sped to the park at top speed, frightening the squirrel from the octopus tree into the branches of a closer elm tree. They'd forgotten to whistle.

The three bicycles parked at Allie's house only ten minutes ago now stood in the deserted park.

Nathan grimaced. "Now what? I'm not much help."

Matt slid off his bicycle and squatted beside Allie's back tire. "First, I'm letting the air out of all their tires. They'll head for them first."

"They'll just take your bike. They like variety."

"I'll let the air out of mine too."

"They'll just run."

"That's where you come in. You stay on the scooter at the gate entrance. If they're really trashing the stations, I may need a witness that I'm not part of them."

"A witness? Don't I have to be alive to do that?"

"I'm going down the trail. I'll film them doing whatever they're doing." He slipped the camera from its case and spotted the phone. "Here."

Once Nathan positioned himself in the gate entrance, Matt disappeared into the wooded ravine side of Boneshaker Trail. The brush picked up every step and breath, but he needn't have worried. Voices and clatter filled the air long before he reached the first check-in station.

Allie, Ball Cap, and Dean struck the site with sticks as if striking a piñata at a birthday party. Matt squatted behind a larger maple tree, put the camera to his eye and pressed his thumb to the red start button.

Allie tore posters into tiny pieces, flinging them high into the air. Dean bashed the fluorescent ropes and Ball Cap the overhead tarp until it fell from its chords.

Ball Cap slumped forward, hands on knees, gasping for breath.

Dean pushed his shoulder. "Come on. Get with it."

Ball Cap wiped a hand across his forehead. "I need some sugar. You have some?" When Dean shook his head, Ball Cap headed for the path. "I have to go to my bike."

Dean scowled with disgust. He slammed his club straight down on a cardboard box.

Ball Cap stumbled down the path, past Matt, with eyes on his feet. Matt moved the camera back to the other two, capturing on film the trashed site. They hiked down the path towards the next station.

Matt waited one long minute. Just as he stood up, a twig snapped behind him. Before he could turn around, a hand tapped him on his left shoulder.

Matt pivoted, left arm swinging out in defence.

CHAPTER 10

SARAH DUCKED.

"S-Sarah!" Matt sputtered. "I thought you were Ball Cap. What are you doing here?" Since both anger at the destruction and relief at Sarah's presence pumped up his internal thermostat, he unzipped his jacket.

"I heard you talking to Nathan at the house and figured you could use some help, but I can probably be more help if I'm conscious."

Embarrassed that he might have slugged his best friend's sister, Matt glanced to the right, then left. "Did you see Ball Cap?"

"I hid in the bushes until he passed. He didn't see me."

"They trashed this station. The other two have gone on to the next." Before he said more, Ball Cap slinked around the bend like an irritating mosquito. He stared straight at them. "Trouble," croaked Matt, realizing their isolation.

Sarah swung around, then sniffed. "I can outrun him."

"Here. Take my camcorder to the Police Station and ask for Officer Ray or Mary. I have the trashing filmed. Tell them I need help."

Sarah slipped the strap over her head and tucked the camera under an arm. "I'm on my way."

Matt watched her skip further into the ravine, making a wide berth to the left of Ball Cap. If he made a move to intercept her departure, Matt knew he'd have to tackle him. The very thought almost buckled his knees.

Ball Cap studied her, but he kept on the path. By the time he stopped a few feet from Matt, a mean spark glowed in his eyes. "You don't know when to stay home, Timmotay."

Breathe in. Breathe out. Breathe in. "Ball Cap, you don't know when to stay out of trouble." Perfect.

Ball Cap's thick eyebrows tightened. He sucked in a rush of air through pursed lips. Then, for what seemed a full half-minute, an ear-piercing whistle charged through the air.

Caught in a stunning time warp where three against one howled impossible odds, Matt thrust his feet forward. Sidestepping the immediate enemy, Matt knew the greater threat stood only a whistle away. His memory exploded with visions of Dean running almost as fast as a racing bicycle.

Ball Cap lunged straight at him.

Matt twisted his shoulder forward and down. A swish of air near his ear marked the closeness of Ball Cap's hand to his collar. Chucking all pride, Matt zigzagged around two slender trees, leapt on the path, and ran for his personal best.

Ball Cap's heavy feet thumping close behind him sent a rush of adrenalin through his veins straight to his feet. Now, his heart pounding against his ribs and thundering in his ears, Matt blinked against the sting in both eyes. The trees blurred. Straining against severe cramps in his thighs, he dared not ease up until he left the trail.

The aroma of fresh donuts greeted him as he sped into the open park. His legs strained the final distance to the octopus tree while he wondered if Tom's baking for the bike-a-thon tomorrow would be in vain . He bent forward, gulping air and pushing down a wave of nausea. Unable to talk, he caught Nathan's eye.

Nathan held up the cell phone. "Battery's dead. Get in the tree."

Sucking in a breath, Matt hiked up the branches. Now, everything depended on Sarah. If nothing else, he may have saved stations three and four.

Ball Cap stumbled from the trail. While he staggered to the tree, his beady brown eyes found Matt. Ball Cap planted a foot on the notch of the tree's trunk. Instinctively, Matt climbed higher by one branch. Ball Cap jumped around on his left foot, then his right.

Ha! Ball Cap couldn't even climb a tree. "What's the matter—" Catching sight of Nathan guarding the park's entrance, Matt clamped his lips together. Nathan couldn't climb a tree now either. Afraid of what he might see in Nathan's face, Matt watched Ball Cap instead.

Ball Cap slumped to the ground with his head between two hands. Matt expected more from the town bully. If Ball Cap thought he would sit it out and let Dean climb the tree, he'd be disappointed. Matt knew the location of four perfect branches for descent. Dean could only manage one at a time.

Then the recruits burst from the trail.

With arms flailing, Dean sped to Ball Cap and thumped him with a muddy shoe. "Get up, you sick bag of bones. You're good for nothing."

"Hey," Matt bellowed. "That's no way to treat a friend."

Scouring the tree, Dean shook his arms out of his jacket. "Come on down, Chicken Little. I've had enough of you. You can die up there or die down here."

Confident the tree gave him safety, Matt declined. "No, thank you. Not today." Allie drew near at a slower pace. She stood a few feet behind Dean. "Allie, you can find better friends than this," reasoned Matt. "Did you hear how he talked to Ball Cap? He even kicked him while he's down. He'll do the same to you, you know."

Allie's eyes, large and dark in a pale face, darted from one to the other.

"Go get the bikes," ordered Dean.

Allie spun around in the direction of the bicycles.

"Ignore him, Allie. He's not going far on his bike."

Dean growled, "It'll take more than the likes of you to stop me from going where I want, Timmotay, so shut up."

Matt rested his arms on a branch in front of him and nodded. "Sure." He watched Allie struggle with the bicycle in the gravel. Flat tires did that. "Looks like you have a slight problem."

Dean's head whirled around to his bicycle. Glaring at Matt, his face reddened and he kicked the front tire of the bicycle. He turned on Allie. "This is all your fault! You're related to all our problems!" As Dean knocked the bicycle to the ground, he spotted Nathan. "Except him." And he dashed towards the gate.

Matt's heart stopped. In seconds, he scrambled out of the tree, but Dean had the advantage. Matt hit the ground, jumped to his feet and sprinted after him. He was half the distance to the gate when Dean grabbed a fistful of Nathan's jacket in his hands and yanked him hard.

Nathan pushed a foot into the space bar beside the scooter's front wheel. One thing about a prosthetic foot, it could snap—painlessly. With an arm under the scooter's handle, Nathan clasped his hands together for strength. He had secured himself on the machine.

A raging yell exploded from Dean, shooting vapour into the chilly air. Dean jumped onto the machine. As he towered over Nathan, Matt clutched two handfuls of the black tee shirt. He pulled until his fingers stung, but the older youth hardly paid him notice.

As Dean shoved a foot in the basket for leverage, Nathan flicked the speed button to rabbit and yelled, "Matt, heads up. We're going to the moon!"

Matt jumped aside.

The purple machine shot forward, spinning round and round in a tight circle. First, Dean's body flopped half over Nathan. He desperately clung to the back of the seat. When Dean shuffled his weight, Nathan eased up on the speed for a second, then sped forward. Nathan steered the scooter in a circle around a dozen times before he stopped.

Dean's head wobbled left as his eyes deviated to the right. His hand wobbled in the air like Jell-o. When he tried to lift his foot out of the basket, Matt jumped forward and strained all his weight on the leg until the foot touched the bottom of the basket again. Dean bellowed, "Help! I'm being assaulted."

Nathan pulled the shoe lace free while Dean struggled to balance on one foot and free the other from Matt's grasp. He was so strong that Matt heaved himself across the basket in order to keep the leg wedged there. Dean bellowed again. "Help. I'm being robbed and assaulted for my shoes! Help me."

Pressure pounded behind Matt's eyes while Nathan knotted the shoelace around Dean's ankle then the steering column. Finally, he nodded at Matt.

Matt eased his muscles, but stayed his position. "Let's talk about how you robbed and assaulted Nathan."

"I never laid a hand on him."

"Oh yes, you did. You had his bike stolen, then you chased him down when he took it back."

"He stole it from me."

"You can't steal something that's yours. And you stole his legs, two of them to be exact. You owe him two legs, cut and sanded."

Dean's sneer wilted, but within seconds his blue eyes iced over.

That coldness pushed Matt's button. "And there's twelve tubes, in the nose, mouth, chest, hands, neck, and other places just to keep him alive. Let's stick those twelve tubes into you, big boy, and take out twenty-two litres of blood because that's how much blood you owe him."

Sirens approached and, although it filled Matt with relief, it made Dean frantic. He pushed Matt with his left hand and yanked his leg up. The knee caught Matt on the chin, and knocked him back. That's when Dean saw the shoe lace knotted around the steering column.

Matt touched his chin, fearful the hit had broken open the recent scar. It stung, but his hand came away clean.

Dean exploded a string of threats. With his hands punching the air, Matt and Nathan ducked this way and that.

Two police cruisers slammed to a stop outside the park entrance. Since Officer Ray arrived first, he cuffed Dean. "You keep yelling like this and you won't have a voice left to talk to your lawyer."

Near the octopus tree, one officer knelt over Ball Cap. "Better call an ambulance. This fellow looks ill."

Officer Mary put a hand on Matt's arm while she talked into her radio. Matt straightened to his feet beside the scooter. Officer Ray asked Matt, "What happened to that one?"

Matt stared at Ball Cap under the tree, his head slumped onto his chest. "Nothing. Dean here kicked him on the leg and called him a sick bag of bones. Maybe he's been sick."

The Officer stared hard at Dean. "Were you doing drugs?"

Dean shook his head, then clamped his lips shut. Whatever Officer Ray asked him, he stared straight ahead as if suddenly deaf and dumb. That is, until the Officer tried to pull him off the scooter and his foot stayed in the basket. Dean hollered in exaggerated agony to the people gathering outside the park's fence. "Help. I'm a victim of Police brutality."

Officer Mary pulled out a camera and snapped a photo of the scooter's basket. "More like the victim of a shoe lace. Where's the girl?"

Allie had disappeared.

MATT AND NATHAN waited for their parents at the Police Station before they gave their statements. Hearing the entire story, Mom cried tears of relief. Matt recognized the disappointment in Dad's eyes when he exposed Allie's part. Two Officers left the station to pick her up.

Well, his Mr. Fix-it days were over. Allie desperately needed help. Her whole family could use some help.

Afterwards, they assessed the damage in the park. Check-in station number one lay in complete ruin. Tattered ribbon met them at the second station. Matt's leg muscles ached. In fact, nearly every muscle in his body hurt. Having seen enough, and with little else to say, they headed home.

Turbo, running circles around Matt, barked and panted. Matt caught him and sunk into a living room chair. While he rubbed the dog's soft ears, Turbo licked his bruised chin.

"Matt, I'll meet you in the garage in five minutes and we'll load up the chairs and coolers into the truck. Afterwards, I think I'll go over to Uncle Ted's."

Matt sneaked a look at him.

Dad winked. "I'm sad about Allie, but I'm fine. Remember what I said before about dealing with this. I want to help Allie."

They had just loaded the last chair into the truck when an unfamiliar maroon truck pulled into the driveway. Matt recognized the burly man from the hospital elevator back when Nathan lay in the Critical Care Unit.

Ball Cap slipped out the passenger side of the truck. Matt's guard zoomed to high alert.

Stretching a hand forward to Dad, the man introduced himself. "I'm Cameron Smith Senior. We've just come from the hospital and we're on our way to the Police Station." Mr. Smith nodded to Matt. "I understand you stood up for my boy."

Stand up for Ball Cap? Maybe in a hundred years when old and confused.

"I heard you," said Ball Cap. "When Dean called me a sick bag of bones."

"Oh-h, that." Matt shrugged. "Dean has to be the worst example of friendship anyone has ever seen."

"Cameron is a diabetic. He takes insulin needles every day, but his body doesn't balance well and he often needs sugar—in a hurry. He could have died there tonight."

Dad's eyebrows shot up. "Did Dean know about the diabetes?"

"Oh yes," said Cameron Senior. "I plan to let the Police know it too. He's a troubled boy, not saying a word about it."

"Come in for a coffee," Dad suggested.

Matt's muscles seized up. Ball Cap in his house? After he had helped trash the bike-a-thon?

"I'm sorry, my wife's due home and I left her a note to meet us at the Police Station. We have to go. I just wanted to say thank you."

Ball Cap punched his hands deep into his jean pockets. "Me too. Thanks. And I'm sorry about messing up the bike trail. I'll tell the police I lied and that you were never part of this."

Smiling at Ball Cap was totally foreign, but Matt forced a little one. "Apology accepted."

After they climbed back into their truck, Matt released one long heavy sigh. Dad clapped him on the shoulder and disappeared into the house.

On Saturday morning, the overcast sky promised rain. Matt secured a new purple collar on Turbo's neck and they headed to Nathan's house. He rang the doorbell and stepped inside with Blue Lightning. Nancy Nadeau swept her arms around both Matt and Turbo. "Good morning. It's a fine warm day." Then she rounded up the older couple, picked up an armful of umbrellas, and hurried to the door. "Sarah's already at the park. We'll see you boys at check-in station three. Good luck."

Matt waved. "See you there." Anticipation charged the air in spite of the heavy atmosphere. After the past several weeks, what could a little rain do?

He found Nathan in his room. Nathan stood up on his legs and set the crutches under his arms. Matt smiled. "Before we go, I have something for you." He handed Nathan the photograph he'd been saving.

Gasping, Nathan stared at the picture for a long time. "Now I remember them. I remember my legs. We were laughing at the squirrel in the tree."

"Thanks to Sarah, you have the best picture in the world of your legs."

"Thanks, Matt. You're the best." He set the photo by his computer, stared at it a moment longer, then wobbled to the hall.

Matt followed him to the scooter and put Turbo into the basket. He rubbed his head affectionately. "I'll meet you out front."

On the way to the park, Matt's success in his part of the bargain grew goose-bumps on his arms. Of course, he'd had the easiest part. Saving Nathan's life and keeping Dad from depression had had the greatest degree of difficulty. "Nathan, do you believe in miracles?"

As they rounded the corner, a rumble of conversation and laughter roared into shouts and waves. Nathan hesitated. Matt gulped, and spoke first. "Where did all these people come from?"

"Do you think it was the newspaper article?"

"Probably," offered Matt. Nathan's eyes sparkled and his smile mirrored supreme satisfaction. The bravery Nathan had shown these past weeks made him proud to be his best friend. "You go ahead," Matt encouraged. "This is your project and they're all waiting for you."

Nathan didn't need to be told twice. Pulling a comb from his jacket, he ran it through his hair. "I do," he answered, "believe in miracles. I am a miracle." He flicked the button to rabbit, put a hand on Turbo, and sped towards the crowd-filled park.

Matt steered Blue Lightning across the street. Tom, standing at the front window, exchanged a wave with him. Matt turned into the alley behind the donut shop and stopped beside the large garbage bin.

Eight weeks of forever had just passed. Forever changed. Forever different.

Grey clouds layered the entire sky, but directly above, one dark cloud hovered lower than the others. As it drifted past, a single drop of rain hit his arm. Behind it, clouds parted and exposed a patch of blue sky. For ten seconds, sunbeams burst through the hole and surrounded Matt with warmth.

His spirit hushed. Peace came. And he whispered, "Thanks."

The bike-a-thon successfully raised over two thousand dollars. Allie moved in with her grandparents for a while and attended family counselling with Uncle Ted and Aunt Kay. Ball Cap signed up for the Young Offenders class. Dean was removed from his brother's custody and placed into Foster Care, awaiting a hearing.